Brow

l

Leighann Dobbs

This is a work of fiction.

None of it is real. All names, places, and events are products of the author's imagination. Any resemblance to real names, places, or events are purely coincidental, and should not be construed as being real.

Other Works By Leighann Dobbs

Lexy Baker
Cozy Mystery Series
* * *

Killer Cupcakes
Dying For Danish
Murder, Money, & Marzipan
3 Bodies and a Biscotti

Blackmoore Sisters
Cozy Mystery Series
* * *

Dead Wrong

Contemporary
Romance
* * *

Reluctant Romance
Sweet Escapes - 4 Romance stories in one book

Dobbs "Fancytales"
Regency Romance Fairytales Series
* * *

Something In Red
Snow White and the Seven Rogues

Table Of Contents

Chapter One

Lexy sat at one of the cafe tables next to the picture window in her bakery, *The Cup and Cake,* admiring how the princess cut center stone of her engagement ring sparkled in the midmorning sunlight. She sighed with contentment, holding her hand up and turning the ring this way and that as she marveled at the rainbow of colors that emerged when it caught the light at different angles.

Her thoughts drifted to her fiance, Jack Perillo. Tall, hunky and handsome, her heart still skipped a beat when he walked in the room even though they'd been dating for over a year. Lexy had met Jack, a police detective in their small town, when she'd been accused of poisoning her ex-boyfriend. She'd been proven innocent, of course, and she and Jack had been seeing each other ever since. And now they were getting married.

Movement on the other side of the street caught her attention, pulling her away from her thoughts. Her eyes widened in surprise—it was Jack! *What was he doing here?*

Lexy felt a zing in her stomach. Jack wasn't alone. Lexy's eyes narrowed as she craned her neck to get a better look. He was with a woman. A tall, leggy blonde who was clinging to him like tissue paper clings to panty hose.

Lexy stood up pressing closer to the window, her joy in the ring all but forgotten. Her heart constricted when she saw how the leggy blonde was pawing at Jack, giggling up into his face. *Who the hell was she?* They looked very familiar with each other. Clearly Jack knew her ... and it seemed he knew her well.

Jack and the blonde started to walk down the street, out of view. Lexy pushed herself away from the window, stumbling over a chair in her haste to get to the doorway. She spun around, righting the chair, then turned, sprinting toward the door.

She reached out for the handle, jerking back in surprise as the door came racing toward her, almost smacking her in the face.

Standing in the doorway was her grandmother, Mona Baker, or Nans as Lexy called her. But instead of her usual cheery appearance, Nans looked distraught. Lexy could see lines of anxiety creasing her face and her normally sparkly green eyes were dark with worry.

Lexy's stomach sank. "Nans, what's the matter?"

"Lexy, come quick," Nans said, putting her hand on Lexy's elbow and dragging her out the door. "Ruth's been arrested!"

"Arrested? For what?" Lexy asked, as Nans propelled her down the street toward her car.

"Nunzio Bartolli was found dead. They think Ruth might have something to do with it!"

Lexy wrinkled her brow. Ruth was one of Nans's best friends. They both lived at the retirement center in town and along with two of their other friends, Ida and Helen, they amused themselves by playing amateur detective solving various crimes and mysteries. The older women were full of spunk and could be a handful, but Lexy had a hard time believing any of them would be involved in a murder. They thrived on *solving* murders, not *committing* them.

"What? How would Ruth even know him?" Lexy opened the door to her VW beetle and slipped into the driver's seat as Nans buckled up in the passenger seat.

"Nunzio was a resident at the Brook Ridge Retirement Center."

Lexy raised her brows. "He was? I heard he had ties to organized crime."

"Well, I don't know about that. He seemed like a nice man." Nans shrugged, then waved her hand. "Now let's get a move on!"

Lexy pulled out into the street, glancing over at the area where she had seen Jack. She slowed down as she drove by, craning her neck to look down the side street where she thought they had gone, but they were nowhere to be seen.

"Can you speed it up? Ruth needs us." Nans fidgeted in the passenger seat.

"Right. Sorry." Lexy felt a pang of guilt. Of course, helping Ruth was more important than finding out what Jack was up to. It was probably nothing but her overactive imagination anyway. Lexy decided to push the leggy blonde from her mind and focus on Ruth.

"So what happened?"

"I'm not really sure. Ida said the police knocked on Ruth's door early this morning and took her in," Nans said, then turned sharply in her seat. "We should call Jack and see if he can help her. Why didn't I think of that before?"

Lexy's stomach clenched at the sound of her fiance's name. She wasn't sure if she wanted to call Jack right now, especially with the image of him and the blonde fresh in her mind. *Should she confront him or let it slide?*

If it was innocent, which it probably was, she'd just make a fool out of herself by confronting him. It was probably a good idea to let some time pass before she talked to him. Lexy was afraid her impulsive nature might cause her to blurt something out she might regret later.

"Hopefully, he'll be at the station. I should call Cassie back at the bakery though, and tell her I've gone out for a while. She'll probably be wondering where I disappeared to." Lexy picked up her cell phone just as she pulled into the parking lot at the police station.

Nans jumped out of the car before she even had it in park. "I'll see you in there."

Lexy watched in amusement as the sprightly older woman sprinted into the station, her giant purse dangling from her arm. She felt sorry for any officer that might try to prevent her grandmother from seeing Ruth.

She made a quick call to Cassie, letting her know where she was and that she'd fill her in later. Then she made her way into the lobby behind Nans.

Nans was talking to Jack's partner, police detective John Darling, who nodded at Lexy as she joined them.

"Ruth isn't arrested!" Nans smiled at Lexy.

Lexy raised an eyebrow at John.

"We just had her in for questioning," John explained.

"Why?"

John rubbed his chin with his hand. "We found her fingerprints and some of her personal effects in Nunzio Bartolli's condo."

Nans gasped. "What? How would those get in there?"

John winked, pushing himself away from the wall he was leaning against. "You'll have to ask Ruth that."

Lexy stared after him as he walked over to the reception desk, his long curly hair hung in a ponytail down his back which swung to the side as he leaned his tall frame over the counter to look at something on the computer. "Actually, she's free to go now. I'll bring her out here if you guys want."

"Please do," Nans said, then turned to Lexy. "Isn't that wonderful? I was so worried."

Lexy nodded as she watched John disappear through the door that led to the offices inside the station. John and her assistant Cassie had been married this past spring and she'd gotten to know him fairly well. She wondered if she should ask him if he knew anything about the blonde she had seen Jack with but didn't want to seem like she was prying into Jack's business.

Lexy shook her head. She needed to stop thinking about the blonde. She trusted Jack. They were getting married, for crying out loud, and she didn't want to be one of those wives who kept her husband on a short leash. The best thing for her to do was to forget all about it.

The door opened and Ruth came out. Nans rushed over giving her a hug. Lexy felt her shoulders relax, relieved that Ruth wasn't in trouble.

"Oh, thanks for coming," Ruth said to Nans and Lexy.

"No problem," Lexy said. "Shall we go? I can drive you guys back to the retirement center, if you want."

"That would be wonderful," Nans said as the three of them made their way to the door. Lexy held it open for the two older women, then followed them out into the summer sunshine.

Ruth breathed in a deep breath of fresh air. "It's good to be outside. For a while there I was a little worried I might be spending my golden years in a cell."

"Why would you think that? Surely you had nothing to do with Nunzio's murder?" Nans raised her eyebrows at Ruth as they walked to Lexy's car.

"Of course I didn't! But they did have some evidence that pointed to me," Ruth said, as she folded herself into Lexy's back seat.

"That's what John said." Lexy slipped into the driver's seat angling the rear view mirror so she could look at Ruth. "What was that all about?"

Lexy saw Ruth's cheeks turn slightly red.

Nans turned in her seat so she could look at Ruth, too. "John said they found your fingerprints and personal effects in Nunzio's condo. How is that possible?"

Ruth turned an even darker shade of red and looked down at her lap, pretending to adjust her seatbelt. "I was in his condo."

"What?" Nans and Lexy said at the same time.

Ruth looked up. Her eyes met Lexy's in the mirror then slid over to look at Nans. "I was seeing Nunzio. Actually, I went there quite regularly. So, naturally, my fingerprints were all over his condo. I was there last night and I must have left a pair of earrings there that the police were somehow able to trace to me."

Nans gasped. "You were there last night? The night he was murdered?"

Ruth nodded. "Yes, I was. But don't worry. I assure you Nunzio was *very* much alive when I left."

Chapter Two

"Why would someone want to kill Nunzio?" Helen slid the cut crystal creamer and sugar bowl over toward Ruth.

Lexy sat at Nans's dining room table, across from Ruth, sipping a cup of freshly brewed coffee. Ida and Helen had been waiting for them in the Lobby when Lexy brought Nans and Ruth back. Now the five of them sat in Nans's condo discussing the morning's events.

"I have no idea," Ruth answered. Lexy's heart clenched when she noticed the other woman's eyes misting over.

Nans must have noticed, too, because she grabbed a box of tissues from the living room and placed them on the table in front of Ruth. "You must be very upset, to have lost your ... friend. I had no idea you and Nunzio were so close."

Ruth grabbed a tissue and blew her nose, then shrugged. "Well, you know how it is at our age. We realize none of us are going to be around for a long time. But to be murdered like that ..." She shuddered, looking up at Ida and Helen. "What happened to him?"

"He was shot. Apparently they used a silencer so no one heard; although most of the people around here are hard of hearing anyway. He was asleep in bed so he probably didn't feel a thing." Ida put a hand gently on Ruth's shoulder.

"One thing is strange, though," Helen said. "His condo was ransacked, as if the killer was looking for something."

Lexy saw Nans's eyebrows shoot up. "Ransacked? I wonder what they could have been after ... and if they found it."

Lexy started to hear warning bells go off inside her head. She could tell when Nans got a bug in her ear about investigating a murder, and it appeared this was shaping up to be one of those times.

"Nans, you're not thinking about looking into this yourself, are you?"

Nans shrugged, but Lexy recognized the bright sparkle in her eye.

"I don't think you should go messing around with this. I heard he had ties to organized crime. This could be related, and that would be very dangerous."

Unfortunately, Lexy's words of warning seemed to pique Nans's interest even more.

"That's right, it could ... I wonder if the mob had him rubbed out?" Nans grabbed her giant old lady purse and started rummaging around inside it. After a few seconds she pulled out an iPad, placing it on the table in front of her.

"What are you doing?" Ruth asked.

"Just looking up some stuff on mob activity."

"You can find that stuff online?" Lexy looked at Nans with wide eyes.

"If you know what to look for." Nans winked at Lexy.

"Well, the man was eighty-five years old," Ida said. "I highly doubt he was active anymore, *if* he was ever in organized crime in the first place."

"Was he?" Nans raised her eyebrows at Ruth.

Ruth waved her hands. "Oh, I don't know. He didn't tell me everything he did, you know."

"Well, can you think of anyone else who would kill him and then toss his condo?" Nans asked, looking back down at the iPad screen.

"Not really. Everyone seemed to like him. It's such a shame. His whole family is in town for a big family reunion to celebrate his eighty-fifth birthday this week."

Nans jerked her head in Ruth's direction. "His whole family? Did everyone get along with him? Did he have a will?"

Ruth looked taken aback. "I don't really know. I wasn't privy to that sort of information," She said primly.

Nans looked up at the ceiling and Lexy could practically see the wheels spinning in her head. Lexy knew she was making a mental list of suspects as well as a list of possible motives.

Now would be a good time for her to leave before she got roped into helping with an investigation.

Lexy went over to the sink and washed out her cup. "I need to get back to *The Cup and Cake*. I left poor Cassie to man the fort alone all morning," she said, making a big show of looking at her watch.

"Oh, wait dear. I was just going to make a list of possible motives ... don't you want to help?" Nans asked.

Lexy squinted at the four older women. "Do you guys really want to get involved in something like this? I mean, if there really is an organized crime connection, then this is nothing to screw around with."

"Lexy might be right," Helen said. "We could end up at the bottom of Brook Ridge falls wearing cement shoes."

Ida looked down at her feet. "Cement shoes? That really wouldn't go with my outfit," she said, causing the four older women to collapse in a fit of laughter.

"Come Lexy, now you sound like Jack. You're not going to turn into a stick in the mud now that you're getting married to him, are you?" asked Nans.

Lexy bristled at the comment. "No ... I just don't want you to put yourselves in danger. Can't you investigate something less dangerous, like who put bubble bath in the fountain downtown?"

Jeez, she really did sound like Jack, she thought, as she heard the words coming out of her mouth.

"Pfft ... that's kid's stuff. Not exciting enough for us."

Lexy sighed. "Well, I really do have to go. I can't tell you guys what to do, but I'm not sure I want to get involved in anything that has to do with Nunzio Bartolli."

"Okay. Well thanks for the ride," Nans said, as Lexy made her way toward the door.

"And for springing me out of jail," Ruth added.

Lexy turned at the door and nodded to the women. "You're welcome. Now try to stay out of trouble." She opened the door slipping out into the hall.

"We'll keep you posted." Lexy heard Helen yell as she closed the door.

Lexy felt her shoulders tense as she hurried down the hall toward the parking lot. She didn't have time to get involved in an investigation right now. She had a wedding to plan and a bakery to run.

Plus, Jack wouldn't be too keen on the idea of her investigating a murder with Nans. He never was, and this time she feared he might be justified—messing around in Nunzio Bartolli's death could prove to be very dangerous.

Chapter Three

"Ruth was sleeping with a mobster?" Cassie held an eclair in the air halfway to her mouth as she stared at Lexy, wide eyed.

"No ... I mean, I don't know. She was apparently involved with this guy and the rumor is he has ties to organized crime. I don't know if that's true or not."

"Oh. Well it sounds like something fishy is going on." Cassie bit into the eclair, making nummy noises that caused Lexy's stomach to growl. In all the excitement, she'd forgotten to eat lunch. Lexy eyed the brownies in the bakery case, then reached in and grabbed one for herself.

Gooey chocolate covered her taste buds as she bit into the confection. The brownie was so fudgy that she didn't even have to chew it. She closed her eyes and swirled it around in her mouth, enjoying the rich, dark chocolate taste as well as the instant sugar rush.

It was mid-afternoon and Lexy realized she probably should eat a proper lunch, but she was having an early dinner with Jack and didn't want to fill up. The brownie was just about perfect, she thought, as she shoved the rest of it into her mouth.

Thinking about dinner with Jack reminded her about the blonde she had seen him with earlier. She *had* tried not to think about it all day, but it kept nagging at her.

Lexy eyed Cassie tentatively. Cassie was married to Jack's partner, who was also his best friend. If there was a reasonable explanation for the blonde, Cassie probably knew about it. More than likely it was something so innocent that Cassie didn't even think to mention it. Lexy was just about to ask when the bell over the door chimed, signaling the arrival of a customer.

Looking over at the door, Lexy saw Brant Millet from the bookstore approaching the pastry case. Brant was tall with a long neck and gangly arms and legs. He reminded Lexy of a giraffe. She suppressed a giggle, picturing a spotted giraffe face on top of his long neck. He studied the case, his chin resting in between his thumb and forefinger.

"What can I get you today, Brant?" Lexy asked.

Brant squinted into the case then pointed at the lemon squares. "I'll take two."

Lexy boxed the squares up and handed Brant the box while Cassie rang up the purchase.

Lexy was considering how to phrase her question about the blonde to Cassie when the bell announced another customer. Another regular, this time a woman Lexy knew only as Susan, who came in three or four times a week. She slunk over to the case, her sleek black hair cascading over her shoulders as she leaned over to examine the pastry. She too, reminded Lexy of an animal ... a black jaguar.

Susan picked out a variety of cupcakes which Lexy boxed up, then rang up the purchase.

Lexy was still thinking about the blonde in the back of her mind, but before she could ask Cassie, the door opened again and two men Lexy had never seen came in looking out of place in dark suits. One was gigantic, tall and wide ... he reminded Lexy of a gorilla. The other very thin, with a long neck and small head, made Lexy think of an ostrich. They ordered a dozen brownies which Cassie boxed up and gave to Lexy to ring up.

The next two hours were filled with a steady stream of customers who cleaned out most of Lexy's inventory while the two girls took turns serving them and ringing up their purchases.

Finally, the rush was over. Lexy glanced up at the clock ... she had just enough time to close up the shop, rush home and get ready for her dinner date with Jack.

Lexy went over to the door and flipped the sign to the "Closed" position while Cassie started cleaning off the cafe tables. Now was the perfect time to ask about the blonde.

"Hey, Cass ... I was wondering if you knew anything about a blonde woman that Jack might know." Lexy feigned disinterest, pretending she was engrossed in cleaning the top of the pastry case, while her heart thumped in her chest waiting for Cassie's answer.

"Uhh ... you don't know?"

Lexy looked up, narrowing her eyes at Cassie. "Know what?"

Cassie stood there staring at Lexy, the wide-eyed, nervous look on her face made Lexy's heart drop.

"Cassie, what is it?" Lexy felt a jolt of panic. *What could be so bad that Cassie didn't want to tell her?*

"That woman you saw with Jack? She's his ex-girlfriend."

Chapter Four

"Should I wear the black dress, or the lavender top and black pants?" Lexy stood in front of the mirror, holding the two outfits on hangers in front of her.

Sprinkles, her white poodle and Shih-tzu mix sat on the bed watching her intently.

Lexy choose the lavender top and slipped it over her head, then wriggled into the tight black jeans. Turning back to the mirror, she angled herself left and right to inspect the outfit from all angles. The top hung just below the waist, accentuating her slim hips, small shoulders, and generous breasts. The pants were just tight enough to show off her assets, but not so tight that she couldn't breathe. She had to admit, she looked pretty darn good.

Staring at her face, she inspected her makeup for smudges. The small amount of dark brown eyeliner and mascara accentuated her green eyes and the teeny bit of blush highlighted her high cheekbones. A swipe of raspberry lip gloss and she was good to go.

"Not too bad, huh, Sprinkles," she said to the dog.

"Woof." Sprinkles wagged her tail.

"I just hope it's enough to make him forget that blonde." She turned back to the mirror, eyeing her brown hair that fell just below the shoulders. Her gaze traveled down her body to her legs which appeared short and stubby compared to the other woman's.

"I know just the thing!"

Lexy opened the door to her walk in closet and headed straight for the shoe rack. She had a weakness for designer shoes and had amassed quite a collection over the years. Her closet was outfitted with special shoe boxes arranged by color. She went to the black section picking out a pair of 6" high Jimmy Choo strappy black suede stilettos. They were sexy and elegant at the same time. She didn't wear them often—they had cost her almost nine hundred dollars—but were worth wearing tonight if it helped her compete with the blonde ex-girlfriend with mile long legs.

Lexy did a mental head shake. She wasn't in competition with anyone. She was way better than some blonde ex-girlfriend. That's why *she* was Jack's fiancee and the other woman was his *ex*.

But, it made Lexy wonder, why hadn't Jack mentioned the other woman to her? Maybe he hadn't had a chance, or maybe it just wasn't a big deal to Jack and he didn't even think it was worth mentioning ... or maybe he was hiding something from Lexy.

Lexy pushed the thought out of her head. That was ridiculous. She trusted Jack. Her imagination was just making a big deal out of nothing.

She grabbed her purse and ran downstairs, Sprinkles hot on her heels. In the kitchen, she peeked out the window at Jack's house which was on the street behind hers. Their backyards abutted each other and she could see his driveway was empty. He was probably on the way over to pick her up.

Lexy threw Sprinkles a treat and dashed out the front door. She was sure Jack would fill her in on the blonde at dinner, but even if he didn't she was determined not to act all clingy and mistrusting. The last thing she wanted was for Jack to know that she was jealous of one of his old girlfriends—if Jack didn't mention the woman at dinner, then neither would she.

Lexy took the top of the bun off her burger, piled onion rings on top of the patty, smothered it in ketchup and dropped the bun back on top. Lifting it she opened her mouth as wide as she could to accommodate the giant sandwich.

Ketchup squirted out the side and dripped down her hands. She wiped it off as she chewed, savoring the delicious combination of sweet onion rings, salty ketchup and charbroiled meat.

Across from her, Jack was creating his own mess by digging into a plate of ribs. He smiled up at Lexy and she felt her stomach flip. Jack had a great smile. Lexy tried not to think about him bestowing that same smile on his blonde ex.

"I guess you must have heard about Ruth," Lexy said taking a sip of her beer.

"Yeah, who knew she had such an active social life?" Jack looked up from his ribs and winked at Lexy, causing her to blush.

"I heard Nunzio was involved in organized crime. Is that true?"

"I don't know. The way he was killed and the way his place was ransacked didn't look very professional to me. He might have been involved with organized crime once, but I don't think his death had anything to do with it."

Jack, put his ribs down and used his tongue to pick rib meat out of his teeth. Lexy watched him thinking he was probably the only man alive who could look sexy doing that.

"So, do you have any suspects? I mean, why would someone kill him like that? I don't like the idea of Nans living in a place where people get shot in their sleep."

Jack shrugged. "Right now we're looking into the family. That's usually the best place to start."

"Really? Why would someone in his family want to kill him? And what would they be looking for in his condo?"

Jack put down his utensils, his honey brown eyes drilling into Lexy's. "I hope you and Mona aren't thinking about investigating this one."

Lexy felt a tingle of annoyance. Jack had an aversion to her investigating murders. She knew it was only because he wanted her to be safe, but it still got her hackles up when he tried to tell her what to do.

Lexy looked down at her burger, removing the top of the bun and cutting into it with a knife and fork. "Don't worry. I have no intention of getting into that. I don't have the time. I even tried to talk Nans out of it, but you know how she is."

Lexy balanced a bit of bun, onion ring, pickle, and cheese covered burger on her fork and carefully lifted it to her mouth. She'd learned through many dinners here, at *The Burger Barn*, that the giant burgers were much easier to eat with a fork, then trying to shove them in your mouth ... even though she still tried the shove-in-your-mouth method every time.

"Yes, I know how your grandmother is—stubborn! Seems to run in the family," Jack teased.

Lexy bristled at the comment even though she knew Jack was teasing. So what if they were stubborn?

Nans and the *Ladies Detective Club*, as the four of them called themselves, had worked on many cases with the police department and had played a critical role in solving several of them. Jack should be thankful for Nans's stubbornness.

She sighed, swirling a piece of onion ring in a puddle of ketchup. She was overreacting. Jack and Nans were old friends, he was practically like a grandson to her and she knew he was very fond of the older woman. This whole thing with the ex-girlfriend must have her out of sorts. Speaking of which ... Lexy was starting to wonder why Jack hadn't mentioned anything about her.

"So ... anything else new going on?" Lexy asked.

Jack narrowed his eyes at her. "New? No, what do you mean?"

"Nothing," Lexy pasted an innocent look on her face, "Just asking if there's anything new."

Jack looked at her sideways. "Lexy, is there something wrong?"

"No." Lexy played with the food on her plate while Jack dug into his ribs as if nothing was amiss. She noticed her engagement ring glinting off the lighting. *Was the ring less sparkly now?*

She took a deep breath. She was acting just the way she had promised herself she *wouldn't* act. *And* she was being ridiculous. She looked around the room. The old barn had a rustic decor, with antique signs and farm memorabilia. A family restaurant, it had comfortable seating and lighting that wasn't too dim or too bright. She and Jack's first date had been here and they'd had many fun dinners here since. She didn't want to ruin that by acting stupid.

She pushed her plate away just as Jack finished cleaning his off. He looked up at her, and for a moment her stomach clenched when she saw concern in his eyes. He was probably wondering why she was acting so strange.

Lexy smiled at him. "Wanna split dessert?"

Jack smiled back, signaling the waitress. "Absolutely."

The Burger Barn had super-sized pieces of cake, and it was a tradition for them to split one at every meal. Jack ordered the double chocolate and asked for two plates and forks.

They sipped coffees and ate the dessert, fighting and laughing over who would get the edge pieces with the most frosting. Just like old times; as if there was no ex-girlfriend waiting in the wings.

When they were done, Jack paid the bill and drove her home. He walked her to the door. Lexy felt unusually awkward as they stood in front of it. She wanted to invite him in, but the image of the blonde draped over him made her hesitate.

Lexy pretended to search in her purse for her keys as she felt the tension grow in the air between them. Jack put his hand on her arm and turned her toward him. Placing his thumb under her chin, he tilted her head up, forcing her to look into his deep golden-brown eyes.

"Are you sure nothing is wrong?" Jack's furrowed brow and concerned eyes made Lexy feel guilty for suspecting something was going on between him and his ex.

Her shoulders relaxed and she smiled. "No. Sorry. It was just a stressful day with Ruth getting pulled in to the police station and all."

Jack nodded. The concerned look in his eye turned to something else as his finger gently traced a line down her neck, past the hollow in her throat and down her cleavage, causing Lexy's heartbeat to kick into overdrive and tingles to race up her spine.

"Aren't you going to invite me in?"

Lexy thought about it. The look in Jack's eye wasn't that of a man who was cheating. If he was, Lexy figured he'd probably want to high tail it out of there, but the glint in his eye told her he intended to stay ... for a long time.

Lexy raised her eyebrow, a smile tugging at her lips. She made a big show of looking at her watch.

"Well, I would, but I do have to get to bed early. I'm bringing day old pastries over to Nans's tomorrow at the crack of dawn," she teased.

Jack's lips formed a smile of their own. He wiggled his eyebrows up and down at her.

"Oh, don't worry," he said. "I'll personally see to it that you get to bed very, very early."

Chapter Five

Lexy put the pastry box that held an assortment of day old pastries from her bakery on Nans's dining room table and opened the lid. Nans, Ida, Ruth and Helen peered into the box.

"Oh, what a lovely assortment," Ida said, choosing a pecan roll.

"You brought my favorite! Pistachio biscotti." Helen gingerly removed one of the crunchy biscuits from the box and put it on her napkin.

"You know I love eclairs. How can I resist?" Ruth bit into the chocolaty confection with gusto.

"Really, Lexy, this is too much," Nans said, picking a cheese Danish out of the box. "All this fatty food will harden our arteries."

Lexy noticed the threat of hardened arteries didn't stop any of them from taking a bite of their pastry as she picked a cream cheese brownie out of the box for herself.

"I've found some exciting information on Nunzio." Nans pushed her Danish aside and pulled the iPad she had sitting on the table in front of her. She tapped a few keys then turned the screen to face the rest of them.

"Look at these newspaper articles. He was arrested quite a few times on various charges but they never stuck. Of course, that was decades ago. But still, I think it proves there could be an organized crime angle to the case."

"All the more reason to stay away from it," Lexy mumbled around a mouthful of brownie.

"Oh. No, dear. That's what makes it exciting!" Nans's eyes sparkled, "Right girls?"

Ruth, Ida and Helen all nodded.

Lexy rolled her eyes. Apparently Nans wasn't going to back off on this one, no matter how dangerous it might be.

"But why would the Mob take him out now? He hasn't been active in that business in a long time," Ruth said.

"Yeah, you'd think they would have had him rubbed out long ago if he was a threat, not wait until he was in his last years," Helen added, with an apologetic look toward Ruth.

"Well, that's just one of my theories," Nans said. "The other one, of course, is his family."

"Right, one should always look to the family first," Ida said. "That's what they do on TV and in the movies."

"Why would his family want to kill him?" Lexy furrowed her brow at Nans.

"Money? Hatred? Revenge?" Nans offered. "You know, all the usual reasons."

"Was there any tension in the family?" Helen asked Ruth. "Did anyone hate him?"

"I don't think so. He never mentioned it. Although he did say some of his relatives didn't live up to his expectations. And he was very disappointed in a few of them." Ruth's brow creased. "Seems to me there were a couple that were always looking for money."

"Aha! That could be a reason for killing him *and* searching his condo!" Ida said.

"I suppose, but that seems rather drastic—especially during a big family reunion week," Ruth said.

"We need to talk to the family. Feel them out. Try to figure out if anyone would have killed him," Helen said.

"Maybe we should have a little memorial here for Nunzio and invite them!" Nans's eyes lit up and she clapped her hands together.

"That's a great idea!" Ida said. "Lexy could cater it."

Lexy's stomach felt queasy. "Oh no," she said holding up her hands, "I don't want anything to do with this."

"Lexy we wouldn't dream of having anyone but you cater it," Nans said. "Think of how good it will be for business."

Lexy wrinkled her brow. She *was* always looking for ways to get new customers. But ending up on the radar of the person who killed Nunzio Bartolli didn't seem like a good way to go about it. On the other hand, she found it almost impossible to say no to Nans.

"I'll think about it."

"Great!" Nans beamed at Lexy.

"We also shouldn't forget about considering the organized crime angle," Ida said.

"Yes, we should put out some feelers to our informants and see if anyone suspicious has come to town in the past few days," Nans added.

They had informants? Lexy narrowed her eyes at Nans. She was about to ask what kinds of informants they had when a police siren outside the window caught her attention.

"What's that?" Ida said getting up to look outside. "Looks like someone's car got broken into."

Everyone rushed to the window. Below, Lexy could see a late model black Lincoln Continental sitting in the parking lot with the front door open. A police cruiser was parked at an angle to it.

A tall, round woman with flashy jewelry and a flowing leopard print top over tight black Capri pants stood next to the car gesturing wildly with her arms. Lexy cast an admiring glance at her impossibly high platform shoes.

"What's she saying?" Helen asked.

Nans unlocked the window and pushed it open so they could hear what was going on.

"This is my father's car. Look at the window —it's been smashed! God only knows what's been taken. I want to know what you are going to do about this!" The woman yelled loudly, standing only inches from the police officer, her hands on her hips.

"Ma'am, please calm down." The officer tried to steer the woman away from the car while the rest of the crew looked inside and performed various tasks that Lexy assumed entailed looking for fingerprints and evidence.

"Hey wait a minute." Ruth pushed Ida and Nans aside so she could get a better look. "That's Nunzio's car!"

Ida narrowed her eyes, craning to see out the window over Ruth's head. "And apparently that must be his daughter."

"This is wonderful news," Nans said, rubbing her hands together.

"It is?" Lexy, Ruth, Ida and Helen all asked at once.

"Of course," she replied. "This means that whoever killed Nunzio and searched his condo is still around. They didn't find what they wanted the first time so they looked in his car. Hopefully, they didn't find it in there either."

"Why do you say that?" Lexy furrowed her brow, her stomach roiled knowing she wasn't going to like Nans's answer.

"Because that means they will keep looking and all we have to do to catch them is figure out where they are going to look next."

Chapter Six

"Nans wants me to cater a memorial service for Nunzio Bartolli at the Retirement Center tomorrow." Lexy straightened up from filling the pastry case in the front of *The Cup and Cake* and turned to face Cassie who was just coming out of the doorway to the kitchen with a tray of fresh, steaming turnovers.

"That sounds like a nice idea. You don't want to do it?"

"Well, you know Nans. She's only doing it so she can pump the relatives for information, to figure out who the killer is."

"Cool! She can have them gathered in one place and then blurt out the name of the murderer like Columbo."

Lexy narrowed her eyes picturing Nans, Ruth, Ida and Helen in beige trench coats with cigars. She noticed Cassie's eyes light up a second before she heard the bell over the door and quickly turned to see who it was.

John Darling stood in the doorway. Of course, she could have guessed who it was judging by the look on Cassie's face. But she never would have guessed he'd have a linebacker with him. At least, that's what the guy standing beside him *looked* like.

He stood about six and a half feet tall and looked almost three feet wide. Lexy could tell from where she stood that he was solid muscle. His expensive looking dark blue suit must have been custom made—she didn't think you could get tree-trunk sized arms like that on suits off the rack.

"Hi honey!" Cassie bubbled.

"Hi." John smiled at Cassie, and then turned to Lexy. "Hi, Lexy."

"Lexy?"

"What? Oh. Hi." Lexy's cheeks burned. She'd been too busy staring at the other guy to pay attention to John's greeting.

"This is Braxton Daniels from the F.B.I. He's in town working on a case with us." John gestured to the giant beside him, then continued. "This is my wife Cassie, and this is Lexy."

"Please call me Brax." The linebacker stuck out a beefy, but well-manicured hand and Lexy watched hers disappear inside it. She looked up into his face. Square jaw, green eyes, smile like a toothpaste model.

She murmured a greeting, and her stomach did a flip when his gaze traveled from her eyes, to her mouth and down the rest of her body, then came to rest on her engagement ring. Right ... she was engaged. No harm in looking though. Lexy withdrew her hand and did her best to send out "not available" vibes.

"So, what kind of case are you working on?" Cassie asked.

"Organized crime. But nothing for you ladies to worry about." Brax tore his gaze from Lexy and looked at Cassie.

"Organized crime? Does that have anything to do with Nunzio Bartolli?" Lexy's radar immediately perked up.

Brax raised an eyebrow at her. "Why would you say that? Do you know something?"

"Well, no. It's just that he was just murdered, and there were rumors about him being connected to organized crime, so ..." Lexy let her voice trail off.

"You made the connection," Brax filled in for her, turning up the wattage on his smile. "So, I guess there's more than just a pretty face under that apron."

Lexy felt her cheeks grow warm and busied herself by taking the turnovers from Cassie and arranging them in the pastry case.

"So you think he was rubbed out by gangsters or something?" Cassie asked.

John and Brax both laughed.

"Well, it's something we are looking in to," John said, then lowered his voice even though no one else was in the bakery to overhear them. "His family isn't above suspicion, either. We are looking at them very closely. In fact, Jack— "

John stopped talking abruptly and Lexy jerked her head in his direction.

"Jack what?"

"I really shouldn't say ... it's part of the case ... he's just keeping the family under surveillance. He's going to be very busy with that."

"Oh. Okay." Lexy narrowed her eyes at John, her stomach sinking. It was more than *just* surveillance, she could tell. What was it that John had stopped himself from saying?

Brax cleared his throat and Lexy looked over at him.

"John tells me you have the best cinnamon buns in the area. I think I'll take that one on top," he said pointing to a gooey cinnamon bun that sat at the very top of the tray.

"I'll take one, too," John said as he walked over toward the self-serve coffee station by the window.

"How do you take your coffee?" He called back to Brax.

"Black." Brax pulled his wallet out of the inside pocket of his jacket and paid for the order. Lexy put the pastries in a white bag which she handed across the counter to him. She noticed he made certain their fingers brushed as she handed off the bag. She pulled her hand back quickly afraid of the tingles that resulted from his touch.

"We gotta run," John said, then looked at Cassie. "See you tonight."

They walked toward the door. When they got there, Brax turned and looked back at them.

"Nice meeting you both," he said, then aimed his gaze at Lexy, "I hope I'll see you again soon." Then he followed John out, shutting the door behind him.

"Wow. Did you get a look at him?" Cassie asked.

"Yeah. How could I miss him?"

Cassie sighed, "Boy, if I wasn't married I'd be wanting to get to know him better."

Lexy laughed. She had to admit Braxton Daniels was attractive. If she wasn't engaged to Jack, she'd have been looking a lot closer herself. But in her rule book, engaged people didn't look around on the side. Her mind conjured up images of Jack and his blonde ex-girlfriend across the street from the day before. She just hoped he was playing by the same rule book.

###

Lexy had her head and shoulders inside the bakery case, stacking a plate of cannoli that she and Cassie had just finished stuffing with rich ricotta cheese filling, when the door opened and Nans, Ruth, Ida and Helen marched into the bakery.

She smiled out at them from inside the case, finished her stacking, then unfolded herself from the awkward position and stood up.

"We thought we would come and pick out what we want to serve at the memorial. It's all set for 2 P.M. tomorrow in the Sunset Room at the retirement center." Nans stared into the case. Her keen eyes scanned the pastries to see what would be most suitable for the occasion.

"How many do you think will attend?" Lexy asked. She could better gauge how many items to bring once she knew how many people would be there.

"Oh, I'd say about forty or fifty people, right Ruth?" Nans turned to look at Ruth who nodded solemnly.

"Then I suggest we do five trays loaded with cookies and bars. I can cut the bars into bite size pieces so people can sample several of them."

"That sounds perfect. We'll take some lemon squares, chocolate brownies, blonde brownies, hermits, chocolate chip cookies, oatmeal raisin, and snicker doodles," Nans said, pointing to indicate each of her choices. "And we'll have some samples to eat here with our coffees."

Lexy cocked an eyebrow at her. "Of everything?"

Nans giggled. "No, just a couple of the brownies cut up will be fine." The four women turned and settled themselves into a cafe table by the window while Lexy cut up the brownies which she brought to the table along with four ceramic coffee mugs.

"... he ever mention any place where he might keep something important?" Lexy heard Nans ask Ruth, as she put the brownies and mugs down in front of them.

Ruth scrunched up her face. "Not that I can recall. We didn't talk about stuff like that?"

"What *did* you talk about?" Ida giggled and Ruth blushed.

"Do you all want coffee?" Lexy asked them.

"Oh, we can get our own. You don't need to wait on us," Helen said grabbing a mug and going over to the self-serve station.

Lexy grabbed a seat pulling it up to the table. She had been lucky to get this storefront in the old mill for her bakery. The floor to ceiling picture window was the perfect place to situate her cafe tables since it had a spectacular view of the waterfall the town was named for. Looking out now, she marveled in the beauty of the water rushing over the falls and the river flanked by shrubs and trees in full bloom. It was no wonder her customers liked to linger at the tables.

"If you were the killer, where would you look?" Nans addressed the table from her spot in front of the coffee carafe.

The other four looked thoughtful. Ida picked a tea bag from the basket on the table and got up to put water in her mug.

Helen looked down at her already steaming coffee and shrugged. "Do you think he could have hidden it in one of the retirement center common areas?"

Ruth and Nans sat back down with steaming mugs of coffee. The smell of dark roast permeated Lexy's nostrils and she got up to pour herself a cup.

Ruth tapped her index finger on her bottom lip thoughtfully. "You know it would be helpful if we knew how big the thing was."

Nans nodded. "What could possibly be important enough for someone to murder Nunzio over?"

"Well, that's easy," Ida said bobbing her tea bag up and down in the water. "It's either got to do with money, or he had something on someone."

Lexy leaned against the self-serve station, the mug of coffee warming her hands. She really shouldn't even be listening to this. She was afraid that if she listened, she would get sucked into investigating with them. Plus the less she knew, the easier it would be to convince Jack that she *wasn't* investigating it.

Nans covered Ruth's hand with her own. "Think hard. Are you sure Nunzio never mentioned anything he was hiding?"

Ruth pursed her lips together. "I don't think so."

"Or gave you something to hide for him?" Helen ventured.

Ruth shook her head. "No. I'd remember that."

"Wait," Ida said. "I'm sure he wouldn't come right out and say that he was giving you some important thing to hide, especially one that was worth killing over. He might have hidden it at your place when you weren't looking or given you something that you don't realize is important."

Ruth sipped her coffee while she thought about it. "Really, we weren't *that* close. Maybe he had another girlfriend he gave it to. The only thing he ever gave me was this locket."

Ruth grabbed a chain that hung from her neck and pulled out a giant heart-shaped locked she'd been wearing under her shirt.

The other woman looked at it and murmured about how pretty it was, even though Lexy thought it was a bit gaudy herself.

"What's inside it?" Ida asked.

"Inside?" Ruth furrowed her brow. "I never thought to look inside."

She wedged her thumbnail in between the two sides and the locket popped open revealing a small key.

"Oh, how cute ... the key to his heart," Ida said.

Nans leaned over the table to get a better look. "Cute my patootie," she said. "That key isn't a piece of jewelry—it's a real key and I bet it opens the lock to whatever Nunzio was hiding."

Chapter Seven

"I have to work late tonight ... on a case. I'm just going to shoot home and grab some leftovers out of my fridge. Maybe we can grill out tomorrow night?" Jack's voice crackled from the cell phone Lexy had pressed to her ear as she pulled into her driveway.

"Sure, that sounds great."

"Okay, well I gotta run. I'll call you tomorrow."

"Bye." Lexy snapped the phone shut. It's not like she was counting on seeing Jack tonight, he often had to work late when a case was heating up. But the last minute notice left her without plans.

"Oh well, such is the life of a police detective's fiancee," she said to herself as she opened her front door.

Sprinkles greeted her in a flurry of white fur as she pushed the door open. Lexy bent down to scratch the little poodle shih-tzu mix's head.

"Looks like it's a girl's night in tonight, Sprinkles."

Lexy dropped her purse on the couch and went straight to the kitchen with Sprinkles hot on her heels. She opened the fridge and pulled out a bottle of white zinfandel, uncorked it and poured it into a crystal wine glass from the cupboard.

Sprinkles danced around her food bowl, alternating looks between the empty bowl and Lexy.

"Are you hungry?" Lexy felt her own stomach nag at her. She filled Sprinkle's bowl from a canister of dry dog food she kept on the counter then opened the fridge to rummage for her own supper.

"Let's see ... leftover carrot cake, tuna, spaghetti and a slice of week old pizza. What will it be?" She stood back with her wine glass in her hand deciding which appealed to her the most. After a few seconds, she grabbed the carrot cake and a fork and sat at the small kitchen table.

The carrot cake was sweet and the cream cheese frosting was tangy, which balanced the sweetness perfectly. Lexy figured she was getting at least two of the basic food groups—vegetables from the carrots and dairy from the cream cheese. The wine wasn't the best compliment to it, but she managed to drain the glass anyway.

Lexy pushed her chair back from the table, then crossed the kitchen to dump the cake plate in the sink. Sprinkles followed her eyeing the space between the plate and ground with hawk-like attention, just in case a crumb fell. Once the plate was in the sink with no hope of a stray crumb falling, Sprinkles made her way over to the door and scratched at it to go out.

"You have to go out?" Lexy asked the obvious. She held the door open for the little dog. Sprinkles wasn't much of an outdoor dog, she usually just went out and did her business then ran back in. So Lexy was surprised when she took off toward the fence that separated her yard from Jack's.

"Sprinkles come back!" Lexy slipped out the door after her, running across the grass in her bare feet. Lexy's heart sank when Sprinkles ignored her and slipped through the missing board in the fence.

Lexy followed, barely squeezing herself through and popped out into Jack's back yard. Sprinkles stood at Jack's door wagging her tail. Lexy ran over to grab her.

She started to scold the dog, but her heart melted when those adoring brown eyes looked up at her and she reached down to pet her instead. She could hardly get mad at the dog, Sprinkles was used to making the trip between the two houses, and Jack spoiled her rotten. It was no wonder she wanted to visit.

"He's not home, silly." A movement inside Jack's house caught her eye. Lexy peered through the window in the kitchen door. A white sheer curtain over the window obstructed the view, but Lexy could make out shadowy movements inside the kitchen.

Didn't Jack say he wouldn't be home?

She pressed her face against the glass to get a better look. Her heart froze in her chest. She could make out two silhouettes ... one looked like Jack and the other was a bit more shapely. A woman.

Just then Sprinkles let out a bark and leaped up against the door. The door swung in causing Lexy to lose her balance. She tumbled into the kitchen face first.

She stumbled a few steps, and then caught herself. Straightening up, a jolt of electricity pierced her heart when she saw who was standing in front of her. She sucked in a deep breath feeling as if the wind had been knocked out of her.

Standing in Jack's kitchen, looking like she was right at home, was the blonde she'd seen Jack with the other day. His ex-girlfriend.

Jack bent down to pet Sprinkles while Lexy and the blonde sized each other up. She was pretty up close, Lexy thought grudgingly, baby blue eyes and blonde hair. A little too much makeup, though.

Lexy's heart sank as she compared the other woman's clingy silk tank top and perfectly matched skirt to her flour covered oversized tee-shirt and jeans. The other woman's outfit was tasteful, but left no doubt that her tall frame carried a body of barbie-doll perfect proportions.

Lexy felt like a dwarf beside her, her curvy but petite frame seemed even shorter than usual considering she didn't have any shoes on to add to her height. To top it all off, the other woman was wearing a gorgeous pair of hot pink Steve Weitzman platforms which made her legs look even longer and her stature even taller.

"What are you doing here?" *Was it her imagination, or did she hear guilt edge into Jack's voice?*

Lexy slid her eyes over to meet Jack's, her heart clenching when she saw how nervous he looked.

"Sprinkles ran over from my house ... I thought you were working?" She glanced from Jack to the woman.

"Oh, I am. I just came home to pick up these leftovers for supper." Jack held up a Styrofoam container. Lexy remembered he *had* said he was going to stop in to pick up his dinner ... apparently he had just forgotten to mention it would be with another woman.

Jack cleared his throat. "Lexy, this is an old friend ... Simone." He gestured to the other woman. "Simone, this is my fiancee, Lexy Baker."

The two women narrowed their eyes at each other as they shook hands. Lexy got the distinct impression that Simone was sizing her up much the same way a snake sizes up its prey, right before it attacks.

"Oh, I didn't know you were engaged." Simone snuck a look at Lexy's ring finger. Lexy wondered if Jack had conveniently forgotten to mention that he had a fiancee or if it simply hadn't come up in conversation.

Jack stood off to the side, fidgeting and running his fingers through his hair.

"Are you working together?" Lexy asked innocently.

"What? Oh, no. Simone just happened to stop by unexpectedly."

"Oh, that was good timing. I mean since you just stopped by the house to pick up your supper."

"Actually, I was waiting for Jack," Simone said. "I'm only in town for a few days and I really wanted to spend some time catching up. I didn't realize he would be working tonight."

You didn't have enough time the other day? Lexy raised an eyebrow at the other woman but was smart enough not to voice her thoughts.

Jack came over beside Lexy. He tried to put his arm around her, but she shrugged him off, bending down to pick up Sprinkles instead.

"Well, I'll let you two catch up then." She turned toward the door without even a look at Jack.

Jack sprinted after her. "Lexy, wait."

Her stomach flipped as he grabbed her by her arm and turned her to face him. Looking up into his eyes, she saw a pleading look pass through them. Lexy wrinkled her brow. This was all very confusing ... on the one hand, it seemed like Jack was trying to reassure her that everything was fine. But on the other, he had an ex-girlfriend in his kitchen.

Lexy didn't know what to think and decided the best course of action was to polish off the bottle of wine she'd left on her kitchen counter before making any rash decisions.

Jack tried to lean in to kiss her, but she was still holding Sprinkles so he couldn't get close enough. Which was just fine with Lexy ... she wasn't sure she wanted a kiss from Jack right now.

"I'll call you tomorrow," He said managing to brush his lips against her forehead. "We're still on for tomorrow night, right?"

"Sure," Lexy said, her stomach plummeting as she walked out the door. She wasn't sure what was going on. She couldn't say for sure that Jack was cheating on her ... it could be all innocent on his part.

But judging by the looks she was getting from Simone, everything wasn't all innocent on *her* part. She could sense a hint of purpose and shrewdness behind those baby blue eyes. Jack might not be doing anything wrong, but Lexy knew one thing for sure ... Simone was up to something.

Chapter Eight

It was ten minutes till two the next day when Lexy finally managed to get the food for the memorial to the retirement center.

"I wasn't sure you were going to make it," Nans said looking at her watch pointedly.

"Sorry. I planned on getting here earlier, but I got a late start today." Mostly due to the bottle of wine I drank last night, Lexy thought.

Balancing two trays of pastry in her hands, she looked around the room. It was furnished with overstuffed arm chairs and sofas. A comfortable room in hues of blue and green, it had a somber tone to it making it perfect for the occasion.

Nans and the ladies had brought in a podium, Lexy assumed for some sort of eulogy, as well as some tables. A few of the tables held photographs of Nunzio in various leisure activities at the retirement center—playing bocce, a bingo tournament and a fishing trip some of them had taken in the spring. The pictures made him look like a regular guy. Looking at the photos, Lexy wondered if he really was involved with organized crime.

Lexy made her way over to one of the empty tables and put the trays down, uncovering them and moving the bars and cookies around to her satisfaction.

"Do you need any help?" Ida asked.

"I could use an extra hand getting the rest of this stuff from my car."

Nans, Ida and Helen followed Lexy out to the car and she handed them the other trays and some napkins and paper plates.

"I was wondering if Jack has let anything slip about Nunzio's case," Nans whispered as they made their way back inside.

Lexy frowned at the mention of Jack's name.

"Not a thing." Then she thought of Braxton Daniels. Thinking about the muscle bound F.B.I agent erased the frown.

"But I did find out the F.B.I. is here looking into it."

Nans swiveled her head around so fast Lexy wondered if she would get a stiff neck. "Really?"

"Yep. He said they're looking into every angle. But he didn't give me any details or anything."

"Oh, darn. You should try to get to know him better to get information out of him. Was he cute?"

Lexy cocked an eyebrow at Nans. "First of all, I don't want to get involved in this investigation and second of all I'm engaged. Remember?"

Lexy watched the tray of brownies Nans was carrying weave and bob as she waved her free hand in the air. "Of course you are. I didn't mean for you to sleep with him, but a little flirting never hurt anyone."

Lexy thought that over as they placed the trays on the tables. She wondered if Jack had the same philosophy. Maybe she should adopt it herself? The thought of getting to know Braxton Daniels a little better wasn't all that unappealing—just for the sake of getting information, of course.

Lexy was glad when people started to file in, interrupting Nans from pressing her further. She busied herself with making sure the coffee carafes were working and the tables were setup properly. She was just about to make her getaway, planning to sneak out and come back a few hours later to clean up, when Nans came over with the woman they had seen in the parking lot the day Nunzio's car got broken into.

"Lexy, this is Gina Ricci. Nunzio's daughter." Nans introduced them and they shook hands.

"Lexy owns *The Cup and Cake Bakery* where all these came from." Nans spread her hands to indicate the pastries stacked on the tables.

Lexy smiled and nodded, eyeing the door and wondering how long until she could sneak off. She had a pounding headache and needed a nap. Turning back to the woman, she watched the dozens of rings on her stubby fingers glitter as she loaded up a small plate with brownies and cookies.

"I'm very sorry about your father," Lexy said.

Gina turned to her and Lexy was almost blinded by the reflection from the gaudy rhinestone necklaces she had layered around her neck.

"Thanks." Gina leaned in towards her and Lexy caught a whiff of stale cigarette smoke and cheap perfume. "Tell ya the truth, I wasn't that close to my father. He was never there for me when I was a kid ... always off doing God knows what. I'm not *that* upset at his passing; except for the fact that no one can find his will."

Lexy heard Nans take in a sharp breath. "I'm sorry, dear. Did you say the will is missing?"

Gina nodded, shifting her makeup caked eyes left and then right. "Yes, he was working on a new will which is missing. The lawyer has his old one, of course. But the new one had some changes. It's causing quite a stir in the family."

Lexy exchanged eyebrow raised looks with Nans as they watched Gina walk away, her black sheer jacket billowing out behind her as she waddled off teetering on six inch high stilettos. *Could the missing will be the reason Nunzio's condo and car were searched?*

"Excuse me. Do these have nuts in them?" A voice at Lexy's elbow tore her attention from Gina and she turned her head coming face to face with a startling pair of gray eyes. The gray eyes were set under manicured brows on a tanned, handsome face attached to a stocky, medium height body and the look they were giving Lexy said they were interested in more than brownies.

"Huh? Oh, no ... they don't have nuts."

"Good, I'm allergic to nuts." Gray eyes shot his hand out toward her. "I'm Barry DeLuca, Nunzio's grandson."

Lexy shook his hand. "Lexy Baker ... I'm just the caterer." She nodded toward the pastry table. "Sorry about your grandfather."

"Thanks," he said, still holding her hand.

Lexy smiled and pulled free from his grasp. She had enough "man" problems without adding this guy to the list.

Barry shrugged. "I didn't get to see much of him growing up and I've been out in Hollywood most of my adult life so we weren't close. I'm an actor you know."

"Oh, that's great." Lexy wondered if he was actually puffing out his chest or if she imagined it. "What have you been in?"

"Well, mostly commercials. A few bit parts in some of the sitcoms," he said picking a brownie from the pile and placing it on a small plate. "I only came back for the reunion. Tell you the truth, I can't wait to get out of here. I forgot how screwed up my family is."

"Really?" Lexy asked.

"Yep." He leaned in closer to Lexy and lowered his voice. "Most of these people didn't even like my grandfather. In fact, I wouldn't be surprised if one of them killed him."

Lexy's eyes widened and she stared at him, trying to decide if he was joking or not. Barry simply nodded at her, took a bite of his brownie, and sauntered off.

Lexy elbowed Nans in the ribs. "Did you hear that?"

Nans turned to her, fiddling with the hearing aid she wore in her right ear. "Sorry dear. I was focused on listening to a conversation over there in the corner." She nodded toward a well-dressed couple in their mid-forties who had their heads together, apparently whispering about something.

"How can you hear them?

"I just turn my hearing aid up ... you can hear all sorts of things you shouldn't with it." Nans smiled at Lexy. "Now, what were you saying, dear?"

"Nunzio's grandson just told me he wouldn't be surprised if one of his relatives killed the old man."

"That's interesting. The couple in the corner apparently weren't big fans of Nunzio. The man is Nunzio's son and the woman his wife. Their conversation made it seem like they were only here to get in his good graces so he wouldn't cut them out of the will."

"You mean the will that no one can find?"

Nans nodded.

"Well, if they're worried about being cut out of the will, maybe some of these others are too?" Lexy scanned the room, wondering if one of them could be the killer.

"We need to find out if any of his relatives needed money," Nans said.

"And which ones hated him enough to kill him." Ruth, who had just joined them, whispered.

"Are all of them here?" Lexy asked.

"Almost. There is one granddaughter—Gina's daughter, I believe, that isn't here yet."

Lexy's cell phone vibrated in her apron pocket. She pulled it out and her stomach flipped when she saw the display, it was a text from Jack, the third one today. He seemed to be overly attentive, probably guilt from Lexy finding him in the kitchen with Simone. Lexy figured she'd answer the texts later today. It wouldn't kill Jack to have to wait and wonder. In fact, it might be good for him.

Lexy slipped the phone back in her pocket with a smile just as she heard a commotion happening over by the door.

"Hi everyone, I hope I'm not too late for Grampy's memorial!"

Lexy glanced over at the singsong voice that cut through the air and her heart froze. Standing in the doorway, in a gorgeous, black designer dress and matching Jimmy Choo rhinestone sandals, was the woman she'd seen in Jack's kitchen last night—his ex-girlfriend, Simone.

Chapter Nine

Lexy was still reeling from seeing Simone at the memorial when she stormed into the kitchen at *The Cup and Cake*.

"You won't believe this!" she sputtered to Cassie who looked up from the task of decorating cupcake tops with one pierced eyebrow raised.

"What?"

"Jack's ex-girlfriend is related to the Mob!"

"Huh?" Cassie put down the spatula and straightened up from bending over the cupcakes, running her hands through her red tipped blond spiked hairdo.

"I just saw her at Nunzio's memorial...she's his granddaughter!"

"Are you sure that was his ex?"

"Yep, I saw her up close at his house last night and then again today. It's the same girl."

"She was at his house?"

Lexy nodded feeling her stomach clench remembering how she had burst in on them. If Sprinkles hadn't run over there, she never would have known.

"That's weird. You aren't thinking...?"

Lexy shrugged. "Well, I really don't know what to think. I've seen them together twice now. If I didn't know how honest Jack was I'd think he was hiding something from me."

Cassie bit her bottom lip. "No. Jack would never cheat on you if that's what you're thinking. John said he wasn't very happy that the ex showed up in town at all."

Lexy pressed her lips together. She didn't want to think the worst of Jack, but she couldn't forget that she'd seen him with Simone ... twice. And those were only the times she'd actually *seen* them. How many other times were there she didn't know about? Her cell phone vibrating in her pocket stole her attention. She pulled it out to look at the display. Another text from Jack. She probably *should* text him back, but making him wait another couple of hours couldn't hurt.

She turned with a sigh. "Well, I better get some baking done. Nans and the girls are bringing my trays back after the memorial and I need to get some brownies made before they show up."

Lexy peeked out into the front room of the bakery. Her part time helper, Haley was busy cleaning off the self-serve coffee station. It was their slow time of day and Haley could handle the customers, giving her and Cassie some time to get the baking done in the kitchen.

She grabbed a large stainless steel bowl from the counter, then assembled the ingredients on the table; butter, cocoa powder, flour, eggs, sugar, vanilla, espresso and salt.

"I still can't picture Jack dating anyone that had ties to organized crime," Lexy said as she melted the butter in a small pan on the gas stove.

"He might not have known she was related. That was a long time ago...before he was even on the police force. You know how it is when you are young. You don't ask a lot of questions." Cassie squinted at the batch of cupcakes in front of her trying to place the silver sugar balls she was decorating them with at precise distances from each other.

Lexy poured the melted butter into the bowl she had on the counter. She supposed that was true.

Was Simone Jack's first love?

Lexy's heart plummeted down to her stomach. No one ever forgot their first love.

"I doubt he still has feelings for her," Cassie said, as if reading her mind. "I mean, how could he possibly be interested in her when he has *you*?"

Lexy's heart warmed and she smiled at her friend. Leave it to Cassie to try to make her feel good. She thought about what Cassie had said as she blended the sugar into the butter.

The truth was that Jack hadn't given her any indication that he *did* have feelings for Simone. In fact, he'd gone out of his way to show her that he *didn't*. And he did make a point of letting Simone know he was engaged to her when he introduced them last night.

She dumped the rest of the ingredients into the butter and sugar mixture working them together with a spatula.

And Jack *did* keep texting her today, which, at least meant he was thinking about her. She was probably reading too much into the whole thing. Lexy resolved to keep an open mind tonight when she went over to his place to grill out.

Lexy looked down at the rich, dark brown mixture in the bowl, and grabbed her secret ingredient ... a bottle of Kahlua. She measured about a quarter cup into the bowl and mixed it in, then took a tasting spoon and scooped up a spoonful.

The brownie mix melted in her mouth, the chocolate was velvety smooth and the espresso and Kahlua gave it a deep, rich taste. Perfect! She put down the spoon and scraped the batter into a pan.

"Yoo-hoo, Lexy! We brought back your trays." Nans appeared in the kitchen doorway, holding her empty serving trays along with a few napkins and plates they apparently hadn't used at the memorial.

"Thanks. You can throw them on the counter," Lexy said over her shoulder as she shoved the brownie pan into the oven.

"Do you have time to take a break, dear? We have a lot to talk about from everything we learned at the memorial, and you have to tell us more about that blonde girl … Simone, was it?"

Lexy rolled her eyes. She could see what Nans was up to. Nans knew she couldn't resist trying to figure things out. Lexy figured the older woman's plan was to keep Lexy in the loop about the investigation thinking that eventually her curiosity would take over and she'd be in the thick of it with them.

But Lexy had other, more important things on her mind right now—like a wedding to plan and an ex-girlfriend to fend off. The problem was that she could never refuse Nans, so she pushed off the counter she was leaning on and followed her out to the front.

###

Lexy poured an extra strong coffee for herself and plopped down in one of the cafe chairs, wishing she'd gone home for a nap instead of coming to the bakery.

"Everyone loved your pastries at the memorial," Ruth said.

"Thanks. How did it go after I left?"

Ruth's eyebrows pressed together adding another layer of creases to her already wrinkled brow. "I was surprised none of his family got up to talk about him. Reverend Peters gave a lovely eulogy though."

"I'm not surprised given what most of them had to say about him," Nans said.

Helen nodded. "Yeah, he wasn't well liked in his own family, but do you think any of them disliked him enough to kill him?"

"I don't know. But some of them seemed concerned about the will. I think a few of them were down and out, and needed money," Ida said.

"We should make a note to look into their finances." Nans turned to Ruth. "Do you have a list of the relatives?"

Ruth nodded.

"Okay, let's find out which ones needed money. The missing will could be a factor too." Nans tapped her bottom lip with her index finger. "I wonder if someone was afraid they were being written out of the will and is looking for it so they can destroy it. Then they would have to revert to his old will ... the one the lawyer has."

Everyone turned to look at Ruth.

"It could be ... he never discussed it with me," Ruth said.

"And we need to find out what type of gun he was killed with, and then see if any of the relatives own that type of gun." Nans looked at Helen with her brows raised.

"That should be easy," Helen said. "I can find out online if any of them had guns registered. Of course, they could still have a gun they didn't register, but there's no way for us to find out about that."

"The way I see it, we have two possible motives. One is that he was killed so the killer could take the will … or whatever it is they are looking for. The other is that someone got mad and killed him in a fit of anger." Nans ticked the items off on her fingers.

"And a third possible motive," said Ida, "is that his involvement in organized crime is what got him killed."

"You mean, like a mob hit?" Ruth asked.

Ida nodded.

"I doubt he was still involved in anything like that …" Ruth let her voice trail off.

"We should still keep it open as an option," Helen said.

"The person who killed him might not necessarily be the one searching for whatever it is they are searching for." Ida took a sip of tea, her keen blue eyes sparkled at them over the rim of the cup.

"Right," Nans said. "He might have been killed for one reason and now his relatives are taking the opportunity to try to find the new will ... or maybe they are looking for something else entirely."

"How much money did he have anyway? It would have to be a lot to be worth killing over, I would think," Helen said.

"That's the thing," Ruth said. "I don't think he had a lot, I mean he never *spent* a lot. I guess I don't know how much he had socked away. For all I know he had a million bucks hidden in various nooks and crannies and that's why everyone is searching his stuff."

"We'll have to look into that," Nans said. "Maybe we can hack into his bank accounts."

Lexy could feel her eyelids getting heavy. She looked out the window, as the ladies droned on about the different possible scenarios surrounding Nunzio's death. The waterfall looked cool and refreshing. People were strolling by on the sidewalk enjoying the summer day, most of them wearing shorts and tee-shirts in summer colors.

Except for the two guys on the opposite side of the street, who seemed to be looking right in the window at them. Lexy narrowed her eyes toward the men. Something was familiar about them ... their dark suits out of place on the hot summer day. Had she seen them at the memorial?

"Lexy!" Nans tapped the table in front of her, startling her.

"Yes?"

"Tell us about Simone. What's she got to do with Jack?"

"He introduced her to me as an old friend, but Cassie said she's an ex-girlfriend."

The ladies eyes all went wide.

"Jack dated someone from the Mob?" Helen asked.

"Well, not really. Simone isn't from the Mob. He probably didn't know the grandfather was—if he even was. Anyway, that was all a long time ago."

Nans narrowed her eyes. "You should try to get more information out of him. I bet he knows something that could be pertinent to our investigation."

"I doubt he would tell me. You know how closed mouthed he can be. Anyway, I don't really want to get involved. Even though I can see that you are trying to drag me in." Lexy smiled at Nans fondly.

"Sorry, dear. It's just that we so love having you in on things with us."

The other women nodded and Lexy felt her stomach clench, then she remembered this was probably part of Nans's plan—make her feel guilty so she'd join in the investigation.

"Let's not forget about the key," Helen said.

"Yes … the key." Nans pressed her lips together. "It's rather small so it must go to some sort of locker or a small box or safe. Maybe even a safety deposit box. We should make a list of all the places in the vicinity that have those types of boxes."

Ruth pulled out the locket and popped it open. "It has a number so that might make it easy for us to find the locker … if it is a locker."

"Shouldn't we tell the police about it and let them sort it out?" Lexy asked.

Nans gave Lexy "the look". "Do you really think the police will take us seriously? A key found in a locket? They'll probably take it and do nothing and we'll never be able to solve the crime. Nope, best to keep it to ourselves ... don't you think girls?"

Ruth, Ida and Helen all nodded.

The bell over the door rang and everyone swiveled their head toward the sound. Lexy felt her stomach flip-flop when she saw Brax walk in. He'd replaced his suit with a black tee-shirt and jeans. The tee-shirt was a little tight, accentuating his perfectly developed physique. Lexy heard Ruth and Helen suck in their breaths.

Brax glanced over at the table and smiled. "Just the person I wanted to see."

Lexy raised her eyebrow, hoping no one could see her cheeks burning and her pulse jumping.

"Oh, are you in the market for another cinnamon bun?"

Brax laughed. His laugh had a deep masculine timbre that sent tingles up Lexy's spine and from the looks on their faces, it had the same effect on Nans and her friends.

"Actually, I hear you ladies know a little bit about the Nunzio Bartolli case," he said looking at Nans, Ida, Ruth and Helen in turn. Lexy notice each woman flushed when his eyes fell on them.

Nans recovered first. "Yes, we do. Ruth here was a good friend of Nunzio's." She pointed to Ruth on the other side of the table. "And who might you be?"

Brax smiled. "How rude of me not to introduce myself. Brax Daniels. F.B.I."

He flashed his badge, then held his hand out and shook hands with each of them as they introduced themselves.

"So, if you're here that means Nunzio's murder must have had something to do with organized crime." Nans narrowed her eyes at Brax.

Brax spread his hands "I can neither confirm nor deny that."

The ladies laughed.

"Seriously, it might not have anything to do with it. That's why I'm here, to figure out whether it does or not. I heard you ladies had some keen investigative skills and I thought you might have some information that would be useful to me."

Ida, Ruth and Helen looked at Nans who stared at Brax, sizing him up. Lexy knew she was trying to decide if he could be trusted and how much to tell him.

"We haven't heard anything about any organized crime connection," Nans said at last. "We had a memorial with the family today and I can tell you there is no love lost between Nunzio and most of them."

Brax raised an eyebrow. "Oh, really? So you think someone in his family might have done this?"

Nans shrugged. "Maybe. We're looking into that angle."

Brax nodded. Pressing his lips together he pulled his wallet from his back pocket.

"Tell you what. If you find anything you think I should know about, give me a call." He handed a business card to each of the women who looked star struck as if he was a rock star handing out autographs.

Nans regained her composure first. "And you'll let us know if you find anything out as well?"

Brax favored her with his sexy, gleaming smile. "Of course."

Lexy stomach somersaulted as he turned his gaze on her and nodded toward the doorway. "Can I talk to you for a minute?"

Lexy got up, wondering why her legs were shaking like a newborn colt. Probably the combination of lack of sleep and caffeine, she reasoned.

Brax pulled her out of earshot, his warm hand on her wrist sending tingles up her arm.

He leaned down talking softly. His lips were close to her ear which made her pulse skitter.

"Your grandmother has quite a reputation as an amateur investigator, but this case could be very dangerous. You'd be smart to get her to back off. I heard she's also very stubborn, so if you can't do that, at least keep a close eye on her. I wouldn't want those sweet old ladies to get hurt."

He stood back just an inch and looked down at Lexy. His green eyes drilled into hers and Lexy thought she saw something more than concern for her grandmother in them.

He tucked a business card into the top pocket of her apron, his fingers brushing lightly against her skin as he did. Lexy's heart jerked in her chest as his gaze went from her eyes, to her lips and then back to her eyes.

"Please call me if anything comes up. Even something that doesn't seem important. Feel free to call me … for anything at all."

He traced his finger lightly down Lexy's arm, then turned and disappeared out the door.

Lexy felt her breath rush out in a whoosh. *Had she been holding it?*

She glanced at the clock and her heart skipped a beat. She only had one hour to close up the shop, rush home, shower, change and then run over to Jack's for supper. Guess that nap wasn't going to happen after all.

Chapter Ten

Jack peered over at Lexy's house while he brushed olive oil on the grill, his heart sinking as he wondered if she was going to show up. He pulled his cell phone out of his pocket and checked the display ... she hadn't replied to any of his texts.

Of course he couldn't blame her for being mad after finding Simone in his kitchen the night before. Jack sighed. He wished he could tell her the truth, but he had to keep it a secret for a while longer.

Jack's heart lurched when he saw her kitchen door open. His pulse quickened noticing she was wearing one of his favorite shirts—a bronze colored V-neck that plunged daringly in the front and highlighted the bronze undertones in her brown hair. The shirt hung loosely over her slim hips. Her mid-thigh white shorts showed off her tanned legs making Jack forget about the two porter house steaks he had been looking forward to grilling all day.

A smile lit his face as he watched her navigate the space from her yard to his, teetering on the grass in impossibly high strappy white sandals, Sprinkles at her heels.

"Hi, there." She greeted him with a smile which Jack hoped meant everything was okay between them.

"Hi." He grabbed her wrist, gently pulling her close. He traced her bottom lip with his thumb, trying to read the look in her eyes, then brushed his lips against hers.

She didn't react.

She didn't pull away, but she didn't fall into the kiss either. Jack didn't know what to make of it, so he released her and turned his attention to the grill.

"Sorry, I didn't reply to your texts today. I catered a memorial for Nunzio Bartolli and time just got away from me." Lexy picked a beer out of the cooler beside the grill and popped it open with a bottle opener. "Can I help with something?"

"Nope. I have everything under control." Jack motioned to the patio table he had already set for dinner. "Have a seat and relax. I'll put the steaks on and I have a garden salad and potato salad in the fridge."

Lexy took a seat and Sprinkles plopped down at her feet while Jack went inside to get the rest of the meal. He opened the fridge and grabbed two large bowls that housed the salads and a platter that had the steak. Balancing them in his hands his stomach clenched as his mind replayed the scene from the night before when Lexy had stumbled into the kitchen to find Simone in here.

Should he bring Simone up or wait for Lexy to do it?

He headed out the door with a sigh, if Lexy asked about Simone, he'd just have to keep with the story of her being an old friend that just stopped by and hope Lexy wouldn't be able to tell he wasn't telling the whole truth.

"That looks delicious." Lexy lifted the Saran Wrap from the salad and picked out a tomato wedge, popping it into her mouth.

Jack shot her a smile then slapped the steaks on the grill, listening to the welcome sound of sizzle as the flames shot up around them. He grabbed a beer from the cooler and sat down at the table.

"So, how was that memorial? I'm sure Mona had ulterior motives for having it." Jack took a long pull on the beer.

Lexy smiled. "Of course. You know her. I didn't stay very long. Just long enough to know Nunzio has some strange relatives."

Jack raised his eyebrows. "You didn't stay? You're not investigating it with her?"

Lexy's brow creased as she took a small sip of beer. "Well, I had no intention of getting involved. But Brax said it could be dangerous and maybe I should keep an eye on Nans. You know how headstrong she can be. Maybe if I help her, I can keep her from doing something crazy that will put her in danger."

Jack narrowed his eyes at Lexy. "Brax? You mean that F.B.I guy? How do you know him?"

"Oh, he's been by the bakery a few times. John introduced us." Lexy casually picked a piece of lettuce from the salad bowl and bit off a dainty piece.

Jack's felt his stomach tighten. He wondered just how many times Brax had been to the bakery. He didn't know the F.B.I agent very well, but he'd heard the guy had quite the reputation with women. He didn't like the idea of him hanging around the bakery ... or Lexy.

"I think the steaks need to be flipped." Lexy nodded toward the grill, pulling Jack from his thoughts. He went over and flipped the steaks with a large fork, then closed the lid.

"Anyway, I'm not really sure what to do. Nans is hell bent on figuring out who killed Nunzio." Lexy looked at him sideways. "Do you have any idea who might have done it?"

Jack took a deep breath. He didn't like discussing his cases and he certainly didn't want Lexy getting involved in this one. The problem was, the more he told her not to the more she would want to. He'd have to be selective about the information he gave her to try to steer her in the least dangerous direction.

"We don't have any solid leads but we *are* looking into the family very seriously."

"Speaking of the family, I saw your friend at the memorial. Simone is it? Did you know she was Nunzio's granddaughter?"

Jack's heart pounded against his ribcage. Lexy knew about Simone. *How should he handle this?*

Trying to shrug casually, he got up to check the steaks. "Yeah, she was in town for the reunion. I didn't know her grandfather was in organized crime back when I knew her. It was a long time ago."

Jack turned to see Lexy looking up at him quizzically and he had to look away fearing she would see he wasn't telling the whole truth. He busied himself with putting the steaks on a platter and placing it on the table.

"Dig in!" He sat down and filled his plate, silently watching Lexy do the same.

Jack's mouth watered as he cut into his steak. It was perfectly seared, the outside brown almost to the point of being crispy and the inside a medium pink. It practically melted in his mouth.

They focused on eating their food for several minutes. The occasional scrape of silverware on plates interspersed with nummy noises were the only sounds to be heard.

Sprinkles danced in between them, shifting her attention from Lexy to Jack. Finally the poor dog could stand it no more and she let out a soft bark, stealing Jack's attention from his steak.

"Oh, you need a treat, don't you?"

Sprinkles went crazy, spinning and bowing. Jack cut a little piece of steak and held it out to the dog who practically rolled her eyes back in her head. She went through a repertoire of tricks—first putting out her paw, then sitting, then rolling over without any prompting—

causing both Lexy and Jack to laugh. Finally Jack gave the steak to the dog who inhaled it, then looked to him for more.

"The steak is delicious." Lexy pushed her plate away and sipped more beer.

"Thanks. I think I have my grilling technique perfected this year." Jack smiled as he popped the last piece of steak in his mouth. Over the past year, they'd grilled out a lot together and he actually had been practicing on cooking the perfect steak.

"Thanks for making all this," Lexy said, as she put the Saran Wrap back over the bowls.

Jack pulled her chair closer to his.

"My pleasure," he said, taking her palm and rubbing it with his thumb, then working his way up her arm, moving his face slowly closer to hers until finally, their lips met.

He kissed her tentatively at first, his heart beat kicking into high gear when she sighed and parted her lips. Her tongue flicked his lower lip and he pressed his mouth harder on hers, scooping her out of her chair and into his lap.

He felt her hands snake around his neck as he caressed the silky fabric of her top, then slid his hands underneath to her warm, soft skin. She let out a mewl of contentment which caused his own growl of satisfaction as a warm tightness started to form in his lower belly. His lips left hers to trail down her neck, his arms tensing to pick her up and carry her inside.

And then her phone rang.

"Shoot." She broke the kiss and looked at her phone on the table. "It's Nans, I better take it." She scrambled out of his lap and back into her chair.

Jack leaned back with a sigh. He watched her answer the phone, thinking of how beautiful she looked with her tousled hair and lips all puffy from their kiss.

But then his heart clenched and his stomach turned to lead when he saw the color drain from her face.

"Lexy, what's wrong?"

She snapped the phone shut and looked at him, alarm in her eyes.

"We have to get to the hospital right away. Ruth's been attacked!"

Chapter Eleven

Lexy's stomach was tied in knots as she rushed down the hospital corridor in front of Jack, her mind conjuring up images of Ruth, tiny and pale, lying in a hospital bed wrapped in bandages.

She skidded to a stop in front of the room. *Where was that loud laughter coming from?*

Peeking into the room slowly so as not to disturb Ruth if she was sleeping, her eyes grew wide and her mouth dropped open.

Ruth *was* propped up in the bed, but she wasn't frail and bandaged. She was sitting in a blue dressing gown, her back supported by several pillows, her cheeks flushed with excitement and her blue eyes twinkling. Nans, Helen, Ida and Ida's fiance, Norman were gathered around the bed. The five of them were having a grand old time laughing and talking.

Lexy looked at Jack who simply shrugged and walked into the room.

"Ruth! Are you okay?" Lexy made her way to the bed and gave Ruth a kiss on the cheek.

"Oh, yes. It takes a lot more than a little crack on the noggin to put me out of commission."

"What happened?" Jack asked from the foot of the bed.

Ruth leaned forward, lowering her voice. "Well, I had just gotten home from the grocery store. The last thing I remember is putting my key in the lock to my condo and BAM." She accentuated the last word by clapping her hands together. "Someone conked me on the back of the head and I went down like a sack of potatoes."

Lexy exchanged worried looks with Jack. "Did you see who did it?"

"No. They hit me from behind. But I must have been out for a while because when I woke up, I was lying on the couch and the house was a mess."

"They searched it?" Lexy's steak sat like a brick in her stomach. If they had knocked out

Ruth and searched her condo, would Nans be next?

Ruth nodded.

"How did you get to the couch?" Jack asked.

Ruth spread her hands. "I have no idea ... and the other funny thing is that my groceries were put away! Which is a good thing because I had ice cream and frozen peas in there."

Jack narrowed his eyes at Ruth.

"This is good news!" Nans said. "If they are still looking for the will, and we know Ruth didn't have it, that means whoever it was is still around and we still have a chance of catching them."

"Did you say they were looking for a will?"

Brax's voice drifted in from the doorway and everyone turned in that direction. Lexy saw Jack's eyes narrow even further and his back stiffen.

"Oh, hi there." Nans craned her neck around the curtain to greet Brax as he walked further into the room.

"I hope I'm not intruding. I heard about Ruth and wanted to make sure she was okay." Brax winked at Ruth whose cheeks turned scarlet.

"Seems I'm no worse for the wear," she said.

"Now what's this about a will?" he asked.

"The family said Nunzio's latest will was missing so we assume that's what they have been looking for." Nans eyed Brax keenly.

Brax rubbed his chin between his thumb and forefinger. "That could be. Or it could be something else... something more dangerous."

"You mean something to do with his days in organized crime?" Nans asked, looking from Brax to Jack.

Brax glanced over at Jack. "We don't know that for certain, but the bottom line is that you ladies shouldn't be messing with this. I'm sure detective Perillo will agree."

Jack nodded. "Ruth wasn't hurt badly this time, but next time you guys might not be so lucky."

Ruth laughed. "Well, I dare say the people behind this can't be all bad. After all they did carry me to the couch and put my groceries away."

"Gentlemen thugs!" Helen said causing a round of giggles.

Brax rolled his eyes at Lexy then pulled her to the other end of the room. Jack followed right behind her.

Brax glanced over at the bed where the others had resumed their conversation.

"Something about this seems off. Why would the family members search Ruth's place?"

"She was Nunzio's girlfriend ... of sorts," Lexy said. "They probably found that out at the memorial."

"What do you think, Perillo?" Brax eyed Jack. From the looks the two of them were giving each other, Lexy didn't think they liked each other very much.

"I agree. Could be someone much more dangerous than a family member. Or the family members could be more dangerous than we thought."

"Yeah ... I'd feel a lot better if Ruth had gotten a look at them. Then we'd have a better idea of who we were up against," Brax said, moving in closer to Lexy. He leaned down toward her, lowering his voice, "I think you better take my advice and keep a close eye on your grandmother."

Jack put his arm around Lexy and she got the feeling she was the prize in some sort of invisible battle. Brax narrowed his eyes at them, his brows rising in realization as he glanced down at her engagement ring.

"She will." Jack answered for her. Lexy wrinkled her brow at him and pulled away. She was perfectly capable of answering for herself.

"Yes, I certainly will," she said, then put her hand on Brax's upper arm. "Thanks for looking in on Ruth."

Brax smiled and turned to leave, giving Jack an unfriendly glare. Then his eyes softened as he aimed them at Lexy.

"You have my number if you find anything out or need my help," he said before turning and disappearing out the door.

"You have his number?" Jack's question forced Lexy's attention away from the retreating back of the F.B.I agent.

"Yes, he gave me his card." she smiled up at Jack. "For the investigation."

Jack furrowed his brow and looked back out into the hall. Lexy wondered if he was jealous of the attention Brax was paying to her. Well, serves him right, she thought. If he can have a woman friend, then she could certainly have a man friend. She figured it wouldn't hurt Jack one bit to see what *that* felt like.

Lexy joined the crowd around Ruth's bed.

"Did you get anything we can use from him?" Nans asked.

"Not really," Lexy replied.

"I think his presence here is a telltale sign this has something to do with organized crime, right Jack?" Helen raised her brows at Jack.

"Not necessarily. We haven't narrowed down all the suspects yet."

"Well, no matter who it is, we know they didn't get what they were looking for from Ruth's place so they will keep looking. I have a feeling this case is about to heat up." Nans rubbed her hands together, a gleam of excitement in her eye.

"Me too," Ruth said, pushing the covers back and swinging her legs over the side of the bed. "Now get me my street clothes. We need to get out of here and start investigating before something worse happens."

Chapter Twelve

"This key isn't the right size for the bus terminal lockers or a post office box." Nans turned the little silver key that had been in Ruth's locket over in her hand, then looked up at the other women. "But I think it might be a good fit for the lockers in the fitness center."

"We could check there first," Ida said. "But I also think we should try to get into Nunzio's condo and see if there is a box or safe with a lock that might fit the key."

"Ruth, you wouldn't happen to have a key to his place, would you?" Nans asked

Lexy saw Ruth blush. "As a matter of fact, I do."

"Okay then, shall we?" Nans stood up and motioned for the others to follow.

Helen, Ruth, Ida and Lexy all pushed themselves away from Nans's mahogany dining table and followed her to the door. Lexy brought up the rear, glad that she had arranged to leave Cassie in charge of the bakery for a few days so she could keep an eye on the ladies and make sure they didn't get into too much trouble.

The fitness center was one building over. They followed Nans down a long corridor, two flights of stairs and through the glass doors that led to the large gym that was free for all seniors who lived at the retirement center.

Nans marched right in heading for the lockers, then stopped short, turning to face the others.

"What's wrong?" Ida furrowed her brow at Nans.

"I just realized Nunzio would have used the men's locker room," Nans said holding the key up. "Who wants to go in?"

The four of them raised their eyebrows and shook their heads.

Nans narrowed her eyes at the desk which was attended by one of the trainers, a twenty-something muscle bound type who was busy frowning over a calendar.

"I'm wondering if you can help me," Nans said approaching the desk.

Muscles looked up with one eyebrow cocked.

"You see, my friend gave me this key to his locker and I need to get his belongings from there." Lexy tried to hide her smile when she saw Nans put her free hand behind her back, her index and middle fingers crossed. "He recently passed away."

"Let me see." Muscles looked at the key then frowned. "This isn't one of ours."

"It's not?" Nans furrowed her brow.

"But if you're friend is Nunzio Bartolli, his brother already came to get the stuff from in his locker."

Lexy felt her stomach sink and saw Nans's brows knit even closer together. "He did? What did he look like?"

"Old guy with a really long, gray beard." Muscles illustrated his words by holding his hand at mid chest level below his chin. "His locker was empty though. Nunzio never kept stuff in it."

"Oh, okay. Thanks." Nans held her hand out for the key and Muscles dropped it in her palm. She turned, raising her brows at Lexy and the others and walked toward the door.

"I didn't know Nunzio had a brother," Nans whispered to Ruth as they walked back into the hall.

"He didn't," Ruth answered.

"He didn't?" Nans narrowed her eyes glancing back at the gym. "Well then who was the guy with the long beard who wanted to look in his locker?"

"I can't imagine who it could be," Ruth said as they followed the hallway out to the covered walkway that led to the detached condos.

"Something doesn't seem right about this." Ida held the big glass door open for the rest of them.

"Did any of you see an old man with a long beard at the memorial?" Helen asked

Lexy shook her head along with everyone else.

"Maybe Longbeard isn't a family member? Maybe he's a mobster," Nans said, her face flush with excitement.

Lexy rolled her eyes as she followed the older women along the walkway. The warm summer air felt good in contrast to the cool air conditioning inside but Lexy didn't have long to enjoy it since she had to jog to keep up with Nans and the gang.

"Maybe we've been barking up the wrong tree the whole time." Nans reached the end of the walkway that spilled out onto a flagstone path leading to a cluster of small condos.

"You mean the family might not have anything to do with it?" Ida asked.

Nans nodded.

"But why would mobsters want the will?"

"Maybe it isn't the will they are after." Nans slowed as a chipmunk scurried across the walkway in front of her.

"Ruth, think carefully. Do you remember if the person who knocked you out had a beard?" Lexy stopped and turned to look at Ruth who pursed her lips in thought.

"No. I don't remember anything … one minute I was taking groceries from the car the next I was waking up on my couch. The doctor said it was common to not be able to remember what happened right before a head injury."

"That's right," Helen said. "The brain has a protection mechanism that disables your conscious memory but your subconscious still knows what happened. And I can tap into that subconscious with hypnotism!"

"That's a great idea," Nans said, "If Ruth got a look at them, she might be able to identify the killer."

Lexy remembered how Helen had hypnotized *her* not that long ago with much success ... and also the added side effect of clucking like a chicken when she drank coffee. She hoped that side effect was worn off by now and made a mental note to look out for it the next time she had some of her favorite brew.

"I guess this one must be Nunzio's." They stood in the courtyard where six detached condo's sat in a U shape. Nans pointed to the one that had a broken strip of yellow crime scene tape hanging down from it.

"I guess it's okay if we go in, seeing as the crime scene tape is broken," Helen ventured.

Ruth stood at the door, rummaging in her purse for a key.

"Are you going to be okay?" Nans put her hand on Ruth's arm and Lexy felt her heart squeeze for Ruth. She had lost a close friend and going in there must be hard for her.

"Oh I'll be fine." Ruth waved her off, produced the key and opened the door.

###

Lexy's heart sank as she stood in the doorway of Nunzio's condo. The place was a mess. Couch cushions ripped open and stuffing on the floor. Cabinet doors hanging and drawers pulled out, the contents scattered about.

"Where do we start?"

The five of them looked around the room in silence. Finally, Nans spoke.

"I guess we should look for a box that might take the size key we have. I'd say it would be about the size of a bread box. Ruth, Ida and Helen, look in here ... Lexy and I will take the bedrooms."

Lexy shivered. The bedroom was where Nunzio had been shot and killed. She followed Nans down the hall, picking her way over the debris. Her gut churned as they approached the bedroom door. She peeked around the doorjamb into the room.

She didn't know why she'd felt so apprehensive. Nunzio's body wasn't there anymore and she'd certainly seen plenty of dead bodies and pools of blood. She should be used to that by now. But still, the chalk outline and dark stain on the rug gave her heart a jolt.

Nans, on the other hand, didn't seem fazed at all. She strode purposefully into the room, looking in the closet and sifting through the debris.

Lexy started over by the bureau. The drawers had been pulled out and the contents lay in a heap on the floor. She poked through the pile. No box.

Getting down on her hands and knees she looked under the bed. Nothing under there.

Lexy noticed a fine black powder over just about every surface; the bureau, the window sills, even the lamps. Finger print dusting powder, she assumed. Looking at her hands she realized she had gotten some on her and wiped it away on her jeans. It was going to be pretty hard not to come out of the condo covered in black dust.

Standing, she surveyed the room. Something nagged at the back of her mind.

Scanning the mess for any bread box sized item her heart jerked when she realized what had been nagging at her. The fingerprint powder was smudged. Not just where she and Nans had been looking but in the other parts of the room.

She went out into the hallway and looked into the guest room which Nunzio had setup as a den. None of them had been in this room yet, which meant the black powder should be visible in fingerprint sized swatches undisturbed. But it wasn't.

"Nans, I think I've found something," Lexy called over her shoulder.

"The box?"

"No, something else. Come here."

Nans appeared in the doorway, her face anxious. "What?"

"We haven't searched in this room yet but look at the black fingerprinting powder. It's all smudged."

Nans scrunched her eyes together and scanned the room.

"So it is." She looked at Lexy wide eyed. "That means someone was in here *after* the police came.

Lexy nodded. "Someone who was searching for something."

"Which means we may be looking for two parties—the people who killed Nunzio and tossed the condo in the first place, and the people or person who came in after the police."

Nans headed back to the living room. "Any luck?"

Helen, Ruth and Ida shook their heads. "Nothing."

"We think someone has been in here since the police ... someone other than the killer."

The three ladies looked up at Lexy and Nans.

"Who?" Ida asked.

"I have no idea. Maybe the brother with the long beard?" Nans answered with a question.

"We need to get a better handle on what it is all these people are looking for," Helen said.

"And find out who had the means, motive and opportunity," Ruth added.

"I did look into some of the things we talked about yesterday." Helen gingerly lifted the corner of a couch cushion to look underneath.

"What did you find?" Nans asked crossing over to the kitchen area.

Helen leaned back on her heels, brushing the dirt from her hands. "I did find that the grandson's all need money as does the son, Lou. That was the gentleman at the memorial who looked like a thug. Several of them do have guns registered. Gina, Lou, and another grandson, Will, who can be ruled-out since he is in the Caribbean on a treasure hunting expedition."

"We still don't know what kind of gun Nunzio was killed with. Lexy, can you find that out, and get the time of death from Jack?" Nans asked.

Lexy's chest tightened. She hated asking Jack investigation details and he never wanted to give them up. She'd have to think of some clever way to get the information from him.

"Sure," she said despite her feelings.

"And I suppose we should start looking into where all the relatives were the night of the murder. We should pay a visit to the daughter, Gina. She might be able to tell us more about the family dynamics and who would benefit from the new will," Nans said

"Or what other things someone might be after," Ida added.

"Most of the family is staying at the Weston Motel. We should head out there after we finish here," Ruth said.

"I agree," Nans said. "Maybe she can clear up some of the questions we have. Lord knows we could use a break in this case."

Chapter Thirteen

Lexy stood outside room 357 of the Weston Motel with Ruth, Ida and Helen and watched Nans tap on the door with her fist.

They heard shuffling noises, a cough and then the sound of the safety chain. The door opened a crack to reveal Gina, her brow furrowed in a question. Then her eyebrows shot up as she recognized them.

"You're the ladies from Daddy's place, aren't you?"

"Yes, we are," Nans said brightly.

Gina's brow creased again. "What are you doing here?"

"We were hoping we could talk to you a bit. About your father."

Gina stepped back, opening the door all the way. "Sure."

Lexy noticed the suite was spacious and clean. A small kitchenette sat off to the left. A hallway, with what she assumed were the bedrooms, was straight ahead. They stood in a newly updated living room with a couch, two chairs and a television. Gina plopped down in one of the chairs and grabbed a cigarette from her pack, then motioned for them to sit.

Nans took the other chair, leaving Ida, Ruth, Helen and Lexy to wedge themselves onto the couch.

"Mind if I smoke?" Gina waved her lighter in front of the cigarette.

"Not at all," Nans answered. Lexy would have preferred no smoke, but Nans had a policy of trying to keep the person they were interrogating at ease.

"This place is nice. And big." Lexy craned her neck toward an open door on the right. "Does that open to another suite or is it all one?"

"We have three suites here, enough for the whole family." Gina made a face. "Well, except my brother."

"Oh, you don't get along?" Nans asked.

Gina exhaled a long stream of smoke. "He thinks he's better than the rest of us."

"Speaking of brothers, did Nunzio have a brother?" Ruth asked.

Gina narrowed her eyes. "No, Daddy was an only child. Why?"

Ruth shrugged. "Someone mentioned a brother. Does someone in your family have a long beard?"

Gina flicked her cigarette ash into the ashtray and frowned at Ruth. "No. Why do you ask?"

"Oh, just a few things we heard, dear, nothing to worry about." Nans leaned over and touched Gina's arm. "We are all so very sorry about your father. Were you all here in the hotel that night?"

"Yes. We were having a big poker game that night. Even my brother Tony came over from his hotel. Daddy had plans with a friend so he wasn't here. But maybe if he had been ..." Gina's voice trailed off and Lexy saw her eyes start to mist.

"Anyway, the game broke up around two. I guess Daddy was already dead by then but, of course we didn't know it yet."

"Has the will turned up?" Nans asked

Gina stubbed her cigarette out in the ashtray. "No. That's why we are all still hanging around here, actually. We're waiting for the police to let us into Daddy's condo so we can look for it ... it's still sealed off for the investigation."

Lexy and Ida exchanged an uncomfortable look. Guess we weren't supposed to be in there, Lexy thought.

Gina continued on, "If the new will doesn't show up, we'll have to go with the last will Daddy gave to his attorney. But I know Daddy didn't want that."

"Oh, really?" Nans prompted.

Gina nodded. "Daddy was kind of a dinosaur when he made that first will. He didn't think much about equal rights for women and such. He felt women were inferior. Which is probably why he got divorced so many times and why I never had a good relationship with him when I was younger." She paused, looking out the window. "But in the past few years, he mellowed a lot. His first will left most of the money to the men in the family ... my brothers and the grandsons. But this new one had equal shares for me and Simone. Daddy told me all about it."

Lexy saw Nans's eyebrows go up. Gina and Simone certainly had a vested interest in finding the new will. *Could one of them have searched Nunzio's after the police were there?*

"So you haven't been looking for the will?" Nans asked.

"Who me? No. Like I said I'm waiting to get access to his condo. I already checked his safety deposit box and it's not in there."

"But somebody searched his condo. And his car," Ida said.

"And killed him," Ruth added.

"They might have been looking for the will ... or something else," Helen said.

"Can you think of anything else your father might have had that someone would have been looking for ... or might have even killed for?" Nans asked. "Maybe something related to his organized crime days?"

Gina wrinkled her brow. "Now that you mention it, Daddy was acting a little strange these past few months." She took another cigarette out of her pack and tapped the end on the table. "He did mention something might happen to him. But at the time I just thought he was worried due to his age. That's why he made the new will. Geez, you don't think he was still in organized crime?"

Nans shrugged. "Does one ever really retire from it?"

Gina put her head in her hands. "He said he was all done years ago." Lexy's heart constricted when she heard the other woman's voice choke up at the end.

Nans reached over and rubbed her arm. "We don't know what happened dear," she said soothingly.

Ida, Ruth and Helen murmured soothing sentiments. Lexy managed to free herself from in between Ruth and Ida on the couch and stand.

"Mind if I use the bathroom?" she asked.

"Oh, sure." Gina pointed to the hallway. "It's down there, the first door is Barry's room, then mine, and the third is the bathroom."

Lexy thanked her and headed down the hall, looking back over her shoulder to make sure no one was watching. She didn't really need to use the bathroom, she wanted the time to do a little investigating. She figured if one of Nunzio's relatives had something to hide, it would be here in the motel. Maybe she'd get lucky and find something incriminating. Like the murder weapon.

Lexy went straight to the bathroom and made a lot of noise shutting the door. Except instead of staying inside, she crept down the hallway and slipped into Gina's room.

The room was neat as a pin. One queen size bed sat against the far wall, the comforter perfectly tucked, pillows plumped. A suitcase stood in the corner. Lexy gave it a quick check but all the compartments were empty. A small bureau under the window held Gina's clothes. Lexy thumbed through them, her heart pounding, her nerves on high alert for any sound out in the hall. She poked around in the desk, the closet and under the bed. Nothing. Finally, she slipped her hand in between the mattress and box spring, but came up empty.

Back out in the hall, she strained to listen to the sounds coming from the living room. The drone of conversation indicated that Gina wasn't going to be getting up any time soon, so she took her chances and snuck into Barry's room.

Unlike Gina's, this one was a mess. Clothes were piled on the floor and one of the twin beds was unmade. Lexy lifted some of the clothes with her foot to see if anything was buried underneath, then gingerly picked up the bedclothes with the tip of her thumb and forefinger.

Lexy's stomach sank.

She wasn't finding anything and she'd been gone a long time. She crossed quickly to the suitcase which lay open on the other bed, clothes hanging out of it in disarray. She rummaged through it but came up empty. The lid had a zipper compartment and she slowly unzipped it so as to not make any noise.

She stuck her hand in, her brow furrowing when she felt something rough in texture. Not the soft fabric of clothing like she expected. She pulled on it, leaning closer to the case as she brought her hand out of the compartment.

Her heart froze.

She stared at the object in her hand—a long gray beard.

Lexy's heart thudded against her ribs as she shoved the beard back into the suitcase. *Barry had been masquerading as Nunzio's brother.*

She crept out of the room, hurried down the hall, quietly opened the bathroom door, then flushed the toilet and made a lot of noise washing her hands.

Trying to stay calm, she walked back to the living room.

Nans looked up at her and she angled her head toward the door, hoping the older woman would get the hint.

"Well, we've taken up too much of your time. We should be going." Nans stood as did Ida, Ruth and Helen.

Gina followed them to the door. "Thanks for stopping by."

Lexy felt like her chest was going to burst as they walked to her car on the other side of the parking lot. She glanced over her shoulder at the hotel to make sure Gina wasn't standing in the door listening.

"You won't believe what I found in there!"

"The murder weapon?"

"The will?"

"No." Lexy lowered her voice, "a long, gray beard."

"What?" Nans's eyes went wide. "You mean Gina was pretending to be Nunzio's brother? I don't see how she could pull that off."

"Not Gina. Barry. At the memorial he told me that he's an actor. I bet he knows how to disguise himself to look to be Nunzio's age."

"But why?" Ruth asked.

Lexy, opened the door to her car, pushing the seat forward so Ida, Ruth and Helen could climb in.

"I know why," Nans said, sliding into the front passenger seat. "Gina said her father changed the will to leave more money to her and Simone. That means the men, including Barry, will be getting *less* money."

Ida snapped her fingers. "He wants to find the will to destroy it!"

"But would he kill Nunzio over it?" Helen asked as Lexy settled herself in the driver's seat.

"Unlikely," Ruth said. "I don't think Nunzio had a lot of money. Not enough to kill over."

"Well if Barry is the one that has been searching for something and he didn't kill him, then who did ... and why?" Ida asked.

Chapter Fourteen

"It seems like we have two parties looking for different things," Nans said as she turned on her coffee pot then took five mugs out of the cabinet. "That's why it's critical that we try to get Ruth to remember who knocked her out."

"If it wasn't Barry, then it could be our second suspect," Lexy said, taking a seat at Nans's dining room table.

"And since the family members seem to all have an alibi for the night Nunzio was killed, it makes sense that someone else is involved." Ida grabbed her iPad and started tapping away. "I have an idea. Give me a few minutes and I might have something."

"Well, even though Gina said everyone in the family was at the hotel having a poker game that night, can we really trust them to corroborate each other's alibis?" Lexy grabbed a steaming mug from Nans. "If they were all in on it, they could easily lie for each other."

"That's a possibility too," Helen said pulling her chair up next to Ruth and taking Ruth's wrist in her hand.

Lexy remembered when Helen had done the same to her, twice actually. The first time it was to help her remember the specifics of a crime scene and the other was to help her get rid of an annoying nervous eye twitch. Both times had been successful, except after the second one she'd ended up clucking like a chicken every time she took a sip of coffee.

Glancing down at her mug suspiciously, Lexy took a sip then looked up to see if anyone was laughing.

Nans looked up at her. "What is it, dear?"

"Did you hear a cluck?"

"No." Nans smiled.

"That's worn off by now, Lexy," Helen said. "Now let's focus on getting Ruth to remember who knocked her out."

They fell silent as Helen worked her magic on Ruth, getting her to relax and then taking her back to when she returned from the grocery store that night.

Lexy sipped her coffee as she watched Ruth, her eyes closed, face relaxed, recount the events.

"I just got back from Market Basket. They had a sale on ice cream so I got two gallons for four dollars plus some other odds and ends. I had two bags which I carried into the building."

"What do you see around you as you are coming in?" Helen asked.

Ruth paused. "Nothing. It's just starting to get dark. Wait! There's someone over near the grove of trees in the parking lot, walking this way."

"What do you do?"

"I'm hurrying into the building. I'm a little nervous. I forgot my pepper spray at home. I should hurry to my condo."

Lexy's stomach clenched for Ruth who was clearly getting a little agitated.

"Ruth, you're safe with us here at Mona's. You don't have to remember any more if you don't want to."

"No. It's okay." Ruth appeared calmer. "I'm at the door to my place ... digging out my keys. Someone is right behind me. Oh!"

"Slow down Ruth, tell us what you see. Remember you're safe."

"There's two of them. But I can't make them out, just shadows. One is a very big man. Tall and wide like a gorilla. The other is also tall, but skinny—lanky with a long neck like an ostrich." Ruth hitched in her breath. "The next thing I remember is waking up on the couch."

"Okay, Ruth. When I tap your shoulder you will wake up feeling refreshed and happy." Helen tapped Ruth's shoulder and her eyes popped open.

"Did you get anything useful?" Ruth asked.

"Sort of," Nans said. "At least we know there are two more people involved and their general description. I don't think Barry fits either one of those."

Lexy wracked her brain comparing Nunzio's relatives to the descriptions Ruth had given. None of them fit, but something niggled at her in the back of her mind.

She let herself relax. A gorilla and an ostrich ... an image of her bakery came to mind and her breath caught in her throat.

"I think I know who they are!"

"You know who the men that attacked Ruth are?" Nans raised her brows at Lexy.

"Well, sort of. I mean I don't know their names or anything but two men who match that description have been coming into *The Cup and Cake* almost every day," Lexy said. "They seem to have an affinity for brownies."

Nans clapped her hands. "That's perfect! All we have to do is hang around the bakery and wait for them to come in. Then we follow them and hope they do something suspicious."

Lexy felt her stomach churn. Somehow following men that knocked out little old ladies and searched their condos didn't seem like such a smart idea.

"We can get some pictures of them and do a photo search on the internet to find out who they are!" Helen said.

"Photo search?" Lexy wrinkled her brow.

"Yes, we can use TinEye or any of the other photo search sites and if a picture of them has been posted, it will come up in the search. So any news articles or even family photos will show up."

"We need to find out what type of gun killed Nunzio because, once we find out who these guys are, we can search the gun registry database to see if they own that type of gun." Nans turned to Lexy. "Lexy, do you think you can try to get that information today?"

Lexy's heart clenched. "I suppose I could visit Jack at the station, but I can't guarantee that he will tell me."

"Bring him his favorite dessert from the bakery," Ruth said. "That will butter him up."

Lexy looked at her watch. She'd have to hurry if she wanted to get to the bakery, pick up a pie and pretend like she was just bringing it to the station on a whim. Maybe it would be easier just to get Cassie to ask John.

Ida interrupted her thoughts. "Speaking of the internet. I've found something very interesting about Nunzio's finances."

"On the internet?" Ruth asked.

"Kind of." Ida winked. "Norman's grandson is a bit of a hacker and ... well ... he helped me take a peek into Nunzio's bank account."

Nans narrowed her eyes at Ida. "Is that legal?"

"No, but wait until you hear. It seems that Barry might have had enough incentive to kill Nunzio over the will after all." Ida paused looking each of them in the eye. "According to his bank account, Nunzio was worth over three million dollars."

Ruth gasped. "That's impossible."

Ida shook her head. "It's true. It's all here." She handed the iPad to Ruth whose eyes widened as she looked at the screen.

"Well I'll be ..." Ruth put the iPad down on the table. "He never let on that he had that much money."

"Not only that, but almost all of it was deposited gradually over the past two years."

"What? But he was retired. On a fixed income."

Ida shrugged. "I know. Makes you wonder what he did to get this sudden influx of money."

"It sure does," Nans said. "And I bet whatever it is was the very thing that got him killed."

Chapter Fifteen

Lexy sat in the police station parking lot watching the top of her coconut cream pie break out in a sweat. It was no wonder, since the sun beating in through the windshield of her VW bug had turned the car into an oven.

She lifted her thick, brown hair off her neck, twisting it into a sloppy ponytail on top of her head. She realized she was procrastinating about bringing the pie to Jack, and wondered why. Probably she was afraid he'd refuse to tell her about the murder weapon and she knew that would make her mad. She felt like she and Jack were already skating on thin ice. She didn't want to rock the boat.

But, if she didn't get out of the car soon, she was going to succumb to heat stroke.

Grabbing the pie, she reached for the car door handle. A movement at the police station door caught her eye.

It was Jack ... and he wasn't alone.

Lexy's stomach sank when she saw who was with him.

Simone.

She saw Simone smile up at Jack. Lexy imagined her batting her eyelashes. *Was he smiling back?* Lexy's heart twitched as she watched them walk out into the parking lot together, toward Jack's truck.

Then she started to feel something else.

Anger.

She had the sudden urge to grab the pie and smash it into Jack's face. But she caught herself just in time. It wouldn't do to get angry like that.

The best way to deal with that sort of thing was to act like she didn't care. For all she knew, it was totally innocent. Right? Maybe it had something to do with the Nunzio Bartolli case and Simone was some sort of witness. Yes, that must be it. Why else would Jack be with her?

Jack's just doing his job, she thought, as she watched them pull out of the parking lot through narrowed eyes.

For a minute she pictured herself following them, just to make sure, then another movement inside the police station caught her eye.

Through the large glass windows in the front, she could see Brax Daniels standing at the desk. The sleeves of his white collared shirt were rolled up to reveal tanned, muscular forearms. From where her car was she could just make out a shadow of stubble on his chin which give him an appealing "bad boy" look.

Lexy looked down at her pie. She wondered if Brax liked coconut cream. *I bet Brax is a lot more generous with sharing information.*

She opened her car door. The outside air seemed cool compared to the roasting stuffiness inside the car, even though it was seventy-eight degrees out. She slipped out of the car, put the pie on the roof, straightened her short denim skirt and fluffed her ponytail, then grabbed the pie and walked over to the police station door.

Cool air rushed out as Lexy opened the door to the station. She stood nervously just inside, the pie balanced in her upturned palm.

Brax turned to look at her, his eyebrows climbing toward his hairline.

"Is that pie for me?"

Lexy held the pie out in front of her and did her best impression of a southern coquette. "Why yes, I do believe it is."

Brax rewarded her with his million dollar smile and walked toward her, causing her heart to flutter annoyingly. He took the pie.

"Coconut cream?"

Lexy nodded.

"I love coconut cream pie." Brax put his hand on the small of her back and swept her out of the reception area and down the hall. He opened the door to one of the interrogation rooms which was now setup as a makeshift office.

"Welcome to my home away from home," he said putting the pie on the table and rummaging in a box on the floor. He pulled out some paper plates and plastic forks. "Aha! It pays to be prepared."

Lexy sat in one of the chairs and watched him cut the pie with the plastic fork and scoop a piece out onto one of the plates. Well, it wasn't actually a piece. It was more like a messy glob. She put her palm up, waving him off when he offered the plate to her. Her stomach was too jittery for coconut cream pie.

Brax shrugged then scooped a large pile onto his fork and sat in the chair on the opposite side of the table.

"Yumm." He closed his eyes and swirled the pie around in his mouth. "This is delicious! Is it from your bakery?"

"Of course." Lexy smiled.

Brax demolished the piece of pie in two more bites then tossed his plate in the trash. Standing, he came around to her side and leaned against the table next to her.

"Now, why don't you tell me why you are really here?"

Lexy felt her cheeks grow warm. It was hard to fool the F.B.I.

He was standing very close to her and she had to lean back in her chair to look up at him which made her feel at a disadvantage. Probably some sort of interrogation technique, she thought as she scooted her chair back a few inches.

"Honestly, I just wanted to drop off this pie."

"For Jack?"

Lexy bit her bottom lip and nodded.

"And ..."

"Nans had a few questions about the Nunzio case."

Brax laughed softly. "And what might those be?"

"We ... I mean she ... was just wondering what type of gun he was killed with and the time of death."

"Oh, well that seems pretty straightforward. You need to bribe Perillo with a pie to get that kind of information?" Brax pushed himself away from the table and walked around to the other side. He grabbed a folder from a pile and rifled through it.

"Says here the time of death was 1:30 a.m. And the bullets were .22 caliber. Probably a revolver."

"Okay. Thanks." Lexy found herself wishing Braxton Daniels would be involved in every case she and Nans investigated. Getting information from him was a lot easier than getting it from Jack.

"Your hair looks nice up like that," Brax said.

Lexy's hands flew up to the hair piled in a mess on her head, her cheeks growing warm. Was it getting hotter in there? She had the urge to get out of there quick.

Lexy pushed her chair back and stood, brushing a wisp of hair out of her face.

"Well, I guess I'll be going. Thanks for the info." She turned abruptly tripping over the table leg on her way to the door.

"Perillo isn't here, you know," Brax said, boxing up the rest of the pie.

"I know."

"He's an okay guy, Lexy. But if you ever get tired of him ..." Brax wiggled his eyebrows up and down and flashed his smile again.

Lexy laughed and fanned herself, reaching for the doorknob.

"Seriously though, your grandmother and her friends might want to back off the Bartolli case for a while. Nunzio wasn't just shot. He was executed. We're dealing with a cold blooded killer here and I wouldn't want any of you to get hurt."

Chapter Sixteen

Lexy shuffled around the pastries in the bakery case as she watched Nans, Ida and Helen sitting nervously at one of the cafe tables. Ruth was out in the back parking lot sitting in her antique Oldsmobile with the motor running. The plan was that as soon as the two suspects appeared in the shop, the rest of them would hop into Ruth's car so they could be ready to follow them.

Lexy brought a tray of cannoli to the table.

"Take some of these and stop staring out the window. You guys look suspicious."

"Oh, sorry dear." Nans turned away from the window and sipped her tea. "You're right, we'll just sit here and nibble just like any other day."

"They probably won't even come in toda—"

Lexy's voice stuck in her throat. The two men were crossing the street, heading straight for the bakery."

"It's them!"

Four gray heads swiveled to stare out the window and Lexy bolted for the back room.

"Cassie, those guys are here. I gotta go."

Cassie went out front while Lexy motioned for Nans and the others to follow her out the back. She'd told Cassie the whole story the night before and Cassie had agreed to stall the men to give Lexy and the ladies time to get in position.

Lexy's eyes narrowed when she saw Ruth behind the wheel of the big, blue car. Her head barely reached over the steering wheel.

Lexy jerked open the driver's side door. "Maybe I should drive. In case it gets hairy."

Ruth wrinkled her brow at Lexy. "I can handle this car, Lexy."

"No time to argue, just let her drive," Nans said sliding into the back seat behind Ida and Helen.

Ruth reluctantly pushed over and Lexy took the wheel, gliding the car out of the parking lot and onto the street where she slid it into a parking spot.

"They're still inside," Nans said. "Helen, get some photos of them."

"Are those the men that knocked you out, Ruth?" Ida asked.

Ruth squinted toward the bakery, her lips pursed in a thin line. "Yes, I think they are."

Lexy looked over her shoulder and noticed Helen was wearing the spy camera glasses the ladies had bought on the internet. They looked like regular eyeglasses but had a teeny camera in them which was perfect for taking pictures without anyone knowing. They'd come in handy on a couple of cases already.

Inside the bakery, Cassie was ringing up the sale. Lexy saw her putting several brownies in a white bag which she handed to the suspects. She put the car in drive while she watched them come out of the store and cross the street, walking up a few cars to a black SUV with tinted windows.

"Is that their car?" Nans asked. "How predictable—bad guys with a black car that has dark tinted windows. Helen, get a picture of the car and license plate."

They pulled out onto the street and Lexy maneuvered out behind them into the light midmorning traffic.

"Stay several car lengths away," Ida said.

"We don't want them to know they have a tail," Nans added. "Once we get past the downtown area, try to stay at least two blocks away."

Lexy rolled her eyes. She knew how to follow someone—she'd seen it done on TV dozens of times.

She kept her distance as they wound their way through town then out to the suburbs. As they got further away from downtown, the traffic got lighter and lighter and Lexy had to fall further behind so they wouldn't be noticed.

"This thing rides nice. You keep it in great condition," Lexy said. Driving the car was like driving a yacht. It sailed down the road and gave a smooth ride. Even though the car was twenty-five years old, it looked brand new. It even had the new car smell to it.

"Thanks," Ruth said. "My Leo bought it brand new. He always kept it up nice. I don't drive it very much anymore, since he passed."

Lexy nodded. Ruth's husband had passed twenty years ago which explained the pristine condition and low mileage.

"Where the heck are they going?" Helen asked.

Lexy felt the uncomfortable flutter of butterflies in her stomach as she followed the black SUV into one of the remote areas of town. Where *were* they going?

"I'm not sure. All that is out here is that old applesauce plant that's been shut down for years."

And that's exactly where they were going. Lexy felt a moment of panic when the SUV turned into the complex.

"What should I do?"

"Drive past. You don't want them to see you follow them in. We'll double back and sneak in later."

Lexy took Nans's advice and drove past the entrance continuing on about a half mile before pulling into a dirt turnoff.

She twisted in her seat to look at Nans. "Do you really think we should go in there? It looked dangerous. And scary."

"Of course. We want to find out what they are up to, right?"

"I guess." Lexy pointed the car back toward the applesauce factory, her heartbeat picking up speed, the closer she got.

The factory was a massive hulk of rusting metal. The remains of two silos stood at one end with a low concrete block building at the other. In between were rows of round concrete structures that stood about seven feet tall interspersed with twisted metal pieces. Remains of the processing plant, Lexy guessed.

Lexy's stomach did a somersault when she saw the SUV on the other side of the concrete structures and she stopped the car. Brax's warning about Nunzio's murder being an execution echoed in her head.

"There they are, over there." She pointed to a space in between two of the concrete pieces where you could just make out the tail end of the car.

Nans twisted around in her seat. "See those bushes over there?" She pointed to an overgrown area loaded with tall bushes at the far end of the lot.

Lexy nodded.

"Head over there and park behind them. I think that will hide us from view."

Lexy headed over taking a route out of the line of vision of the SUV. She pulled in behind the bushes and Nans jumped out, heading for a small space in between two shrubs. Helen produced a pair of binoculars from her purse and followed Nans with Ruth, Ida and Lexy close behind.

"Yep, it's them all right." Helen pulled the binoculars away from her face and handed them to Nans.

"Yep." Nans passed them to Ruth.

"He's even eating one of the brownies." Ruth passed them to Ida.

"Chocolate frosted. He's got some on his lip," Ida said passing the binoculars to Lexy.

Lexy could see the two men just fine without binoculars. They were standing beside the SUV as if they were waiting for someone. The tall skinny one held the bag of brownies in his hand. The large one was stuffing the second half of a brownie in his mouth, which was smudged with frosting.

"What are they doing?" Ida asked holding her hand out for the binoculars.

"Looks like they are waiting for someone." Nans pushed her head further through the bushes and squinted.

"I think you're right." Helen pointed toward the road where a black mid-sized car had turned into the entrance to the factory.

"What is it with the black cars?" Ruth asked.

"And the tinted windows," Lexy said. The car had a dark tint on the windows making it impossible to see who was inside.

The five of them watched in silence as the car pulled to a stop beside the two brownie eating thugs.

Lexy held her breath as the driver's side door opened. A long, bare leg appeared outside the door—a woman's leg ending in an expensive pair of Jimmy Choo stiletto's with a metal heel. The woman belonging to the leg slithered out of the car and Lexy felt her heart jerk in her chest.

"Simone!"

"Shhhh …" Nans waved her hand, but she needn't have worried. They were too far away to be heard.

Lexy watched as Simone approached the two men. She pointed to her mouth and the big thug wiped the brownie smudge off his lips. Lexy couldn't make out what she was saying, but judging from the way her hands were gesturing wildly in the air, she wasn't happy.

Finally, she stormed off in the direction of the concrete building, the two men following on her heels.

"Did you get pictures of that?" Lexy asked Helen.

"I sure did."

Lexy pulled out her cell phone.

"What are you doing?" Nans grabbed her arm.

"We need to call Jack and tell him about this," Lexy said.

"Tell him about what? That we saw three people go into a building?"

Lexy bit her lip. Nans had a point. Jack would probably just yell at her for meddling. And since Simone was one of the three people, that made it even sticker. Lexy didn't want it to appear as if she was trying to get Simone in trouble because she was jealous.

"We need to get some hard evidence before we call in the police," Helen said.

"Right," Nans said, heading back to the car. "Let's go back to my place and run those pictures through the internet and see what comes up."

Ruth didn't let Lexy drive on the way back which was just as well since Lexy's head was reeling with questions about Simone meeting with the thugs. What was she up to? Did Jack know about it?

Back at Nans', they gathered around her dining room table while Nans hooked the camera glasses to her computer with a USB cable. Lexy watched as she uploaded the pictures to the internet, then used a sophisticated online picture search to try to match the men in the photos to any pictures currently online.

"Bingo!" Nans turned to face them from her seat at the computer table. Her face was flushed with excitement as she pointed to an image on the screen.

Ida walked over to the computer, bending down and squinting at the monitor.

"These guys are definitely with organized crime," She announced.

"Looks like the fat one is called Louie The Finger. I wonder why that is?" Nans asked. "Here's an article on a restaurant hit that he was suspected in."

Lexy shivered despite the warm temperatures in Nans's condo. These guys *were* killers.

"And the skinny one is Sal Toreo. Skinny Sal," Ida said.

"Let's run their names through the gun registry and see what they have for guns."

Nans worked the keyboard and a list came up on the screen.

"Looks like Louie has a lot of guns. Including a Colt .22 caliber." Nans snapped her fingers. "Yep, this is our guy!"

"Okay, so we can be reasonably sure they killed Nunzio. But why did they search his condo and Ruth's?" Ida asked.

"And where do Barry and Simone fit into all this?" Helen added.

Nans tapped her lips with her index finger. "That's a good question. Barry and Simone have opposite goals when it comes to the will. She would want it to be found and he would want to destroy it."

"So they probably aren't working together," Lexy said.

"Right, but Simone *is* working with Louie and Sal." Nans tapped Sal's face on the computer for emphasis.

"Yeah, and I wonder what they are up to." Lexy narrowed her eyes at the computer.

"Well, they obviously have something inside that abandoned factory," Nans said to Lexy. "I think you, me and Ruth need to head on over there tomorrow and take a look while Helen and Ida do more research."

"I don't know. That sounds pretty dangerous." Lexy's stomach clenched at the thought of poking around inside the old factory.

"There's got to be a clue inside that we can give to the police. We'll wait until they leave and then just take a peek. We won't be but a few minutes. It will all be totally safe, I assure you. Can you pick us up at eight?"

Lexy could see Nans was aiming her most honest, trustworthy look in her direction, but it did nothing to stop the butterflies from flapping around in her stomach. Everyone was looking at her expectantly, though, and she didn't want to seem wimpier than a bunch of old ladies. Plus she knew Nans and Ruth would just go without her anyway, and she wanted to be there in case they got into trouble.

Lexy let out a sigh. "Okay, eight o'clock it is, then."

Chapter Seventeen

Lexy squinted through the binoculars she had trained on the entrance to the applesauce factory. The squinting combined with the glare of the sun was giving her a headache, and she was beginning to wonder if Louie and Sal were ever going to leave. She felt a flurry of relief, chased by a pang of nervousness, when she saw their black SUV finally coming up the entrance driveway.

"They're leaving!"

"Let's wait until they've gone down the road a ways. We don't want them to see us going into the factory in the rear view mirror," Nans advised from the passenger seat.

Lexy started the engine and let it idle, handing the binoculars to Ruth in the back seat who trained them on the road.

"Okay, hit it!" Ruth said after a few seconds and Lexy pulled out onto the road heading toward the factory, her heartbeat picking up speed the closer she got.

She drove straight to the place where they'd seen the two thugs and Simone go into the building and parked the car.

"I guess this must be the door." Ruth pointed to a rusted metal door set into the concrete block building.

Lexy tried the knob. It turned. She opened the door and peered inside.

"It's kind of dark in here. Do either of you have a flashlight?"

Lexy turned to see Nans rummaging in her purse. "You're bringing your purse in? Wouldn't it be easier to just leave it in the car?"

"Oh no dear, I bring this everywhere. You never know when you might need something. Like this flashlight," she said producing a small, round cylinder from the depths of her bag.

Lexy turned it on and aimed the light into the building. The inside was covered in years of dust and dirt. Several thin windows let streaks of light in at the end of the building which was one large room with several offices sectioned off to the side.

Lexy stepped in. It was hot inside and smelled like mildew and old dirt.

"Let's start in the offices over here." Nans's voice beside her made her jump.

"Okay. Be careful of those boards." Lexy trained the flashlight on the various loose boards and piles of sheet rock that littered the floor as Nans navigated the area with a vigor that belied her age.

The three of them went into the first office which had a rusty metal desk, some filing cabinets and chairs.

"This office has been used recently," Ruth said as she squatted down level with the desk. "There's no dust on the surfaces."

Nans opened the filing cabinet and Ruth started poking in the desk drawers while Lexy held the flashlight up to illuminate the room for them.

"What are we looking for, anyway?" Lexy asked as a dust mote flew up her nose causing her to sneeze violently.

"I'm not sure exactly. Anything that has to do with the case. I think we'll know when we see it. Once we find something, we can get out of here and hand it over to Jack and let the police handle the arrest."

Lexy alternated between pointing the flashlight at Ruth and Nans. She was busy directing the beam into a drawer that Ruth was inspecting when she heard the sound of a rusty door hinge from Nans's direction.

"Bingo!"

Lexy turned her attention in the direction of Nans's voice. Her grandmother was standing in front of a metal locker, the open doors revealing a cache of guns inside. But instead of the look of accomplishment she expected to see, Nans's face looked surprised, her eyes wide.

"Uh-oh," Nan's said looking at something behind Lexy.

Lexy's heart jerked.

She whirled around to see what was behind her but her vision was obstructed by a large, beefy hand with dark hairy knuckles coming toward her face.

Before she could react, her nose and mouth were covered by something soft and sweet smelling.

Struggling to breathe she kicked out at her assailant.

Then everything went dark.

Chapter Eighteen

Lexy's hips and shoulders pressed against the hard floor. Her head pounded and she felt nauseous. She squinted one eye open in the dimly lit room. *Where was she?*

"She's coming round." Lexy heard a voice. *Was that Nans?*

Someone helped her sit up and she held her head in her hands willing the spinning to stop. After a few minutes, she felt better and lifted her head.

"Are you okay, dear?" Nans peered at her nervously.

"I think so." Lexy did a mental scan of her body. Other than the headache, she felt fine. The nausea was almost passed and the pounding in her head was dissipating.

"What happened?"

Nans grimaced. "The thugs discovered us in the office. They chloroformed you and dragged us all into this storage room. We're locked in."

Lexy looked around the room. It appeared to be some sort of store room with metal shelves along the back and sides. There were no windows, but a sliver of light came in from under the door allowing her to see the basic outlines of things in the room.

Lexy's heart lurched when her gaze fell on Nans and Ruth. The two women were seated in plastic chairs to her right. In the dim light she could just make out that Nans had a tear in the bottom of her shirt and Ruth's face was smudged with dirt.

"Are you both okay? Did they hurt you?"

"Oh, we're fine. They didn't hurt us. My shirt caught on the metal desk and Ruth was already dirty from poking through the office," Nans said, then turned to Ruth. "You know, you have dirt smudged all over your face."

Ruth looked startled. "I do?" She immediately started digging in her purse coming up with a napkin she used to wipe her face.

"You have your purses? What about your cell phones? We could call for help." Lexy felt the cloud over her heart lift with hope.

"No such luck," Ruth said. "They took our cell phones and yours too."

"Otherwise, we would have signaled for help already," Nans said. Then her face brightened.

"Wait a minute." She picked up her big old lady purse from the floor and dug around inside. "They took our cell phones, but they didn't take the iPad!"

"What's Jack's email?"

"Email? He doesn't use email ... can't you call him on that thing?"

"Not unless he has another apple device with FaceTime." Nans frowned. "Oh, I know."

Lexy watched Nans dig in her purse again, this time coming up with a business card, holding it in the air like it was a trophy.

"What's that?" Lexy asked.

"Brax Daniels's business card," Nans said, squinting down at the card while she held the iPad at an angle to cast light on it. "Oh good, he has his email listed."

While Nans was busy typing an email on the tablet, Lexy ventured over to the door. She grabbed the knob, pushing and pulling. It wouldn't budge. She threw her shoulder against the door. Still nothing.

"We already tried all that, dear," Ruth said, then turned to Nans. "Did you try FaceTiming Ida? If there's a strong enough signal out here for that we could get her to call Jack and tell him where we are."

"I'm trying now," Nans said, looking anxiously at the device while it made hollow ringing sounds.

Lexy walked over behind Nans and looked over her shoulder, her stomach roiling and shoulders tense, willing Ida to answer. The ringing stopped and Lexy felt the tension leave her shoulders when Ida's face filled the screen.

"Mona? Where are you? It's so dark I can hardly see anything."

"We've been captured by the thugs!" Nans said in a loud whisper.

"What? Where ... you ..." Ida's voice was fading out.

"Ida? Are you there? I can't hear you."

Ida's face flashed on the screen, then off and Lexy felt her stomach drop when the screen flashed a note about a bad connection.

"Damn!"

"It's okay dear, I'm sure Brax will get that email soon and—"

Nans's words were interrupted as the door to the room burst open. Lexy's heart froze in her chest when she saw Louie The Finger and Skinny Sal rush in through the open door, guns drawn and pointed in her direction.

"What's all da racket in here?" Louie yelled his eyes growing wide when he saw the iPad in Nans's hands.

Lexy's heart thudded as Louie advanced on Nans who sat wide-eyed in the chair.

"Gimme dat," Louie said, pointing at the tablet.

"Yeah, hand it over. We don't wanna have to rough youze ladies up," Sal added.

Nans handed the iPad to Louie who wrinkled his brow at it. "Dis is one of dem dere computers, ain't it?"

Nans nodded and then shrugged. "There's no reception here so it's not much good."

Louie narrowed his eyes at Nans. "I hope you didn't call da cops on dis thing."

"Oh no, you can't use it as a phone, unfortunately." Nans gave Louie her most innocent look.

"We ain't takin' no chances." He handed the device to Sal. "Put dis in da' office."

Lexy eyed the open door as Sal left with the iPad. *Could she overpower Louie and make a break for it?*

"Now don't go gettin' no ideas." Louie waved his gun toward Lexy as if he knew what she was thinking.

Lexy stepped in front of Nans. "What do you want?"

"Youze know what we want," Louie said. "Da list."

"List?" Nans furrowed her brow. "What list?"

"Da one Nunzio had," Sal said from the doorway as he rummaged in one of Lexy's white bakery bags, coming up with an oversized fudge brownie. Bright light spilled in from the open doorway making it easy for Lexy to see the details of the storage room and read the expressions on the thugs' faces.

"We don't know anything about any list. Is that what you guys have been looking for?" Ruth asked.

Louie's heavy black brows knit together. "Don't act dumb wid me. We wouldn't wanna hurt youze nice ladies now. Would we Sal?"

"No siree." Sal swallowed a big chunk of brownie, then gestured toward Lexy with what was left of it. "Hey, ain't that da brownie lady?"

Louie stepped closer. "Yeah, da one from da bakery."

"I hope we don't have to kill her. I really like dese brownies."

Louie gave Sal a threatening look. "Will you stop with the brownies and pay attention, here?"

Louie turned his attention back to Lexy and Nans.

"Now you listen up. We wanna know where dat list is hidden, or dis one is gonna get it." He jabbed a finger threateningly in Nans's direction and Lexy's heart shrank.

"But we don't know about any list," Ruth said. "We thought you were looking for the will."

"Will? What will?"

"Nunzio's will. It's missing." Ruth shrugged.

A look of confusion crossed Louie's face and he glance back at Sal. "Da boss didn't say nothin' 'bout a will, did she?"

She?

Sal swallowed the last of his brownie and shook his head. "Nope."

Louie turned back toward Ruth pointing his finger at her. "Don't you be tryin' to throw us off track. We know youze ladies know somethin'."

"Really, we don't," Lexy said.

"You shut it!" Louie yelled turning his pointer finger toward her and Lexy shrunk back. With all this finger pointing, Lexy wasn't surprised the guy's nickname was "Louie The Finger".

"What was on this list, anyway?" Nans asked. "Maybe if we knew, we'd be able to tell you if we saw it."

Louie narrowed his eyes at her. "You don't know?"

Nans shook her head.

Louie looked back uncertainly at Sal.

"Tell 'em," Sal said.

"Nunzio had a list of retired crime bosses and dae crimes dey never got busted for. We need to get it."

Lexy inhaled sharply. So *that* was what they were looking for. No wonder they were going to such great lengths. A chill ran up her spine when she realized that was the type of list someone would kill for.

"What about da key?" Sal tilted the open brownie bag toward Louie who shook his head.

"Yeah, we saw you wid a key when weze was watchin' youze in da bakery before. I bet it opens da box dat has da list," Louie said to Ruth.

Too bad no one knows where that box is.

"Oh." Ruth self-consciously pulled out her locket.

"Is it in dere? Hand it over," Louie said gruffly.

"Well I don't know what it goes to." Ruth looked uncertain.

Lexy felt a jolt of electricity pierce her heart as Louie took two steps in Ruth's direction, reached out for the locket and yanked it off the chain.

"Ouch." Ruth rubbed her neck.

"Sorry. Youze need to do what we say, otherwise I might hafta hurt 'ya." Louie shrugged then turned the locket over in his palm. He brought it closer to his face, squinted at it and tried to pry it open with his thick thumb.

"Let me." Sal held out his hand and Louie dropped the locket in. Sal pried it open with his two thumbs and the key popped out.

"Here it is," he said holding the key in the air.

Lexy held her breath. *What would they do with them now that they had the key?*

"What's it go to?" Louie asked.

"That's the million dollar question," Nans said. "We have no idea."

"We better wait for da boss to come and see what she thinks," Louie said.

"What about dem?" Sal thrust his chin out toward Nans, Lexy and Ruth while he pocketed the key.

"We'll see what da boss wants us to do wit dem," Louie said, pointing his gun toward them, causing Lexy's stomach to tumble. "No funny stuff while we're gone."

The two of them backed out of the room closing and locking the door, leaving Lexy, Nans and Ruth in darkness.

"What do we do now?" Lexy whispered as her eyes tried to adjust to the sudden dim light.

"Hopefully Brax will get our email and send in the troops," Ruth answered.

"We're not just going to stay here like sitting ducks," Nans said, "I have a plan."

"You do?" Lexy asked.

"Of course I do," Nans answered. "Ruth, can you fake a heart attack?"

"What? Why I suppose so. Why would I do that?"

"To create a diversion."

Lexy narrowed her eyes at Nans, her heartbeat picking up speed. *Just what was her grandmother up to?*

"Ruth, do you have a can opener in your purse?" Nans asked while rummaging in her own purse.

"A can opener? Why I just might." Ruth bent down and picked up her purse. Setting it in her lap, she opened it and started feeling around inside.

"What do you want a can opener for?" Lexy asked.

"I noticed that there are dozens of cans of applesauce on the back shelves there." Nans waved her hand in the direction of the back of the room.

Lexy's eyes were adjusting to the low light and her gaze followed the direction Nans had indicated. She noticed row upon row of large applesauce cans sitting on the shelf, covered in inches of dust and mottled with rust.

"Those are decades old. They're probably no good anymore!" Lexy's stomach clenched thinking about the nasty contents of the cans. "Surely you can't be that hungry?"

"We're not going to eat them, dear," Nans said, then turned to Ruth. "Ruth, did you find a can opener?"

"Yes! Here it is." Ruth held something up.

"Great." Nans leaned in toward them and whispered. "Okay, now, here's what I want you to do."

Chapter Nineteen

Ruth lay on the floor about five feet inside the room, clutching her chest and moaning loudly.

Nans and Lexy banged on the door.

"Help us! She's having a heart attack!"

They heard Louie and Sal running toward the room and jumped back just before they threw open the door.

"What's all the commo—" Louie started to say, then his eyes went wide as he slid on the thick layer of applesauce that Lexy, Nans and Ruth had spread out in front of the door. Sal was right behind him and couldn't stop in time.

Lexy's heart hammered in her chest as she saw their feet slip up in the air, their legs flailing as they both landed flat on their backs in the slippery sauce. It would have been almost comical, if they didn't have guns.

Ruth was up in a flash, holding her gigantic purse that was now filled with heavy applesauce cans. She started pummeling Louie in the head with her purse while Nans did the same to Sal, knocking both the men out cold.

Lexy grabbed their guns and the three of them gingerly stepped over the applesauce and made a bee line for the main exit.

Nans got to the door first. Lexy saw her reaching for the handle, then her heart jerked in her chest as the door exploded inward and Brax Daniels along with five of Brook Ridge Falls finest came barreling through, guns extended.

"BRFPD. Put your hands in the air!"

Ruth and Lexy stopped in their tracks and raised their hands, but Nans simply brushed off her shirt and straightened her back.

She walked right over to Brax.

"We've already captured your suspects and have them immobilized for you in that room over there." Nans nodded toward the storage room, then continued out the front door with a look of satisfaction on her face.

Brax looked at Lexy while the rest of them ran for the storage room. "What happened?"

"You probably won't believe this, but Nans captured them with applesauce." Lexy held up the two guns. "These are their guns, and there's a locker full of more guns in one of the offices."

Brax laughed as he took the guns "Applesauce?"

"Yep. You'll see. But they mentioned that their boss was coming. A woman," Lexy said.

"Yeah, we caught her outside. Jack's arresting her right now." Brax looked over toward the office where Louie and Sal were. "Why don't you head on out, but stick around. We'll probably need to question the three of you."

Lexy's heart clenched when she saw Jack with Simone just outside the door. She stood there with her mouth wide, her heart sinking. It looked like Jack had his arm around her.

She was just about to turn away and join Nans and Ruth when Jack turned and saw her.

"Lexy. Thank God you're okay!" Jack shoved Simone toward the police car and that's when Lexy noticed he didn't have his arm around here—he was handcuffing her!

Her stomach flip-flopped as she watched him cram Simone in the back seat, bonking her head on the roof in his haste. Then he turned and jogged over to Lexy. Her heart melted as he took her in his arms.

"I was so worried about you when Brax told me he got Nans's email."

"You were? But what about Simone?" Lexy looked back at the police car uncertainly. "I thought she was an old friend."

"Simone? She was. Sort of. But that's not why she was here in town."

"No?"

"She's with organized crime. She's behind Nunzio's death." Jack pushed a lock of hair behind Lexy's ear.

"But she was his granddaughter!" Lexy felt her heart constrict for Nunzio.

"Yeah, she's not a very nice person."

"But she was at your house … and …"

Jack put his finger on Lexy's lips. "Shhh. That was all surveillance work. I was trying to get vital information from her."

"You were?" Lexy wrinkled her brow. "But it looked like …"

"I know." Jack pulled her in even closer. "I wanted to tell you that I was only hanging around with her to find out what she was up to and to feed her false information, but I didn't want to jeopardize the case."

Lexy looked into his honey brown eyes and her heart melted. "Really?"

"Of course," Jack said, "You know you're the only one for me."

And before Lexy could answer, he lowered his lips to hers causing her to forget all about Simone, organized crime, and applesauce.

Epilogue

"So, Gina finally found the new will," Nans said, as she bit into a white frosted chocolate brownie.

"Yep." Ruth nodded. "She mentioned that Nunzio had given her an engraved silver box the night before he was killed, but the box was locked and she couldn't get it open."

"And the key from the locket fit?" Lexy wiped the crumbs from the table and brought a fresh pot of coffee over.

"Yep, I brought the key over and we popped it in, and the will was inside." Ruth smiled at the memory. "It gave her a share of Nunzio's millions that was equal to her brothers. She was very happy."

"No doubt." Lexy pulled out a chair and sat at the table. Glancing out the front window she marveled at how refreshing the waterfall looked and how bright the day was. Especially in contrast with being locked up in the applesauce factory.

"What about the grandson that was pretending to be Nunzio's brother—he couldn't have been very happy to see the new will surface," Ida said.

"Oh, he wasn't," Ruth answered. "Started yelling about how it wasn't fair. Gina was very upset. I didn't have the heart to tell her what he'd been up to."

"And I suppose he won't be prosecuted for anything. I guess he really didn't commit much of a crime. So we'll really never know if he was the second person that searched Nunzio's condo," Ida added.

"It's too bad the granddaughter turned on Nunzio like that," Helen said.

"Yes, thankfully Jack got the evidence to put her behind bars for a long time, right Lexy?"

Lexy blushed at Nans's words. She felt bad that she had thought Jack was fooling around when the whole time he was digging up evidence on Simone. He'd known she was a crook all along.

"Yeah. She thought she was playing cute and using him for information, when it was really the other way around!" Lexy laughed, the glitter from her engagement ring catching her eye and making her heart swell.

"But she really wasn't the mastermind. Just another hired henchman," Ida said over the rim of her coffee cup.

Ruth nodded. "The other retired mob bosses hired her to silence Nunzio and get the list. Then she hired Louie and Sal."

Nans snorted. "Louie and Sal weren't all that bad. I'll never forget the looks on their faces when they went down in the puddle of applesauce."

Everyone at the table laughed.

"Yeah, I felt kind of bad they took them to jail. They were nice enough to put my groceries away after they knocked me out," Ruth said. "Then again, they *were* the ones that actually killed Nunzio, so maybe we don't want them loose on the streets."

"Did anyone ever find the list?" Helen asked.

"It hasn't surfaced yet," Jack said as he joined them at the table. "But we're still looking for it. A list like that could be very valuable to us."

"And to the retired mobsters. Which explains how Nunzio got those big deposits of money the past few years," Helen said.

Jack's eyebrows mashed together. "How did you find out about that?"

Helen just winked at him and took a sip of her coffee.

"Yep. Nunzio just went down the list, blackmailing each mob boss one after the other. It was a great plan, really. I mean it's not like the other mob bosses were going to tell the police on him," Nans said.

"Yeah, a good plan, except it got him killed." Ruth rolled her eyes.

"Now, I'm sure I don't need to tell you ladies that you played a very dangerous game with this one." Jack looked pointedly at Nans.

"Well, we did get our man and managed to escape relatively unscathed," Ruth said.

"Yeah, but next time you might not be so lucky." Jack aimed his gaze at Lexy and her stomach flip-flopped. "I know you like to investigate and we appreciate the help, but I'm a little upset you put yourselves in danger by going to the applesauce factory. That wasn't very smart."

Lexy felt her cheeks grow warm and looked down at the table.

"I hope you won't do anything that dangerous in the future." Jack picked up Lexy's hand, looking at her shiny engagement ring. "I need my bride-to-be in one piece for the wedding."

Nans smiled. "Oh don't worry dear. We've had enough investigating for quite some time. Haven't we girls?"

Ruth, Ida and Helen all nodded.

"In fact, we're planning a nice vacation in the mountains. Rustic cabins, a big lake, fine dining and all the activities we could want."

"That sounds nice," Jack said. "Maybe you can scout out honeymoon places for us." Jack looked at Lexy and raised his eyebrows causing giggles from everyone at the table including Lexy.

"We may at that." Nans smiled at Jack. "I'm planning for it to be a peaceful vacation far away from things like blackmail and murder. After all, what could possibly happen at a rustic retreat in the woods?"

The End.

Lexy's Brownie Recipe

This recipe includes two of Lexy's secret ingredients - Kahlua and coffee. It's rich and fudgy, just the way Louie and Sal like them.

Ingredients:

4 ounces unsweetened chocolate

1/2 pound butter, unsalted

2 tablespoons instant coffee

2 cups sugar

1/4 cup Kahlua

1 teaspoon vanilla extract

5 eggs

1 cup all purpose flour

1/2 teaspoon salt

Preparation:

Preheat oven to 350F.

Melt butter, chocolate and instant coffee on low heat. Whisk until smooth. Remove from heat and let cool until it is luke warm.

Whisk in sugar, Kahlua and vanilla.

Add eggs, one at a time, whisking thoroughly after each egg.

Whisk the flour and salt together, then add to the chocolate mixture.

Spread batter in a 13 x 9 inch pan and bake for about 35 to 30 minutes until a toothpick inserted in the center comes out clean.

A Note From The Author

Thanks so much for reading my cozy mystery "*Brownies, Bodies and Bad Guys*". I hope you liked reading it as much as I loved writing it. If you did, and feel inclined to leave a review over at Amazon, I really would appreciate it.

This is book five of the Lexy Baker series, you can find the rest of the books on my website, or over at Amazon if you want to read more of Lexy's and Nans's adventures.

Also, if you like cozy mysteries, you might like my book "*Dead Wrong*" which is book one in the Blackmoore Sisters series. Set in the seaside town of Noquitt Maine, the Blackmoore sisters will take you on a journey of secrets, romance and maybe even a little magic. I have an excerpt from it at the end of this book.

This book has been through many edits with several people and even some software programs, but since nothing is infallible (even the software programs) you might catch a spelling error or mistake and, if you do, I sure would appreciate it if you let me know - you can contact me at lee@leighanndobbs.com.

Oh, and I love to connect with my readers so please do visit me on facebook at http://www.facebook.com/leighanndobbsbooks or at my website http://www.leighanndobbs.com.

Are you signed up to get notifications of my latest releases and special contests? Go to: http://www.leighanndobbs.com/newsletter and enter your email address to signup - I promise never to share it and I only send emails every couple of weeks so I won't fill up your inbox.

About The Author

Leighann Dobbs lives in New Hampshire with her husband, their trusty Chihuahua mix Mojo and beautiful rescue cat, Kitty. She likes to write romance and cozy mystery novelettes perfect for the busy person on the go. These stories are great for someone who doesn't have a lot of time for reading a full novel. Why not pick one up and escape to another time and place the next time you are waiting for an appointment, enjoying a bath or waiting to pick up the kids at soccer?

Find out about her latest books and how to get her next book for free by signing up at:

http://www.leighanndobbs.com

Connect with Leighann on Facebook and Twitter

http://facebook.com/leighanndobbsbooks

http://twitter.com/leighanndobbs

<u>Other Works By Leighann Dobbs</u>

Lexy Baker
Cozy Mystery Series
* * *

Killer Cupcakes
Dying For Danish
Murder, Money, & Marzipan
3 Bodies and a Biscotti

Blackmoore Sisters
Cozy Mystery Series
* * *

Dead Wrong

Contemporary
Romance
* * *

Reluctant Romance
Sweet Escapes - 4 Romance stories in one
book

Dobbs "Fancytales"
Regency Romance Fairytales Series
* * *

Something In Red
Snow White and the Seven Rogues

Excerpt From Dead Wrong

Morgan Blackmoore tapped her finger lightly on the counter, her mind barely registering the low buzz of voices behind her in the crowded coffee shop as she mentally prioritized the tasks that awaited her back at her own store.

"Here you go, one yerba mate tea and a vanilla latte." Felicity rang up the purchase, as Morgan dug in the front pocket of her faded denim jeans for some cash which she traded for the two paper cups.

Inhaling the spicy aroma of the tea, she turned to leave, her long, silky black hair swinging behind her. Elbowing her way through the crowd, she headed toward the door. At this time of morning, the coffee shop was filled with locals and Morgan knew almost all of them well enough to exchange a quick greeting or nod.

Suddenly a short, stout figure appeared, blocking her path. Morgan let out a sharp breath, recognizing the figure as Prudence Littlefield.

Prudence had a long running feud with the Blackmoore's which dated back to some sort of run-in she'd had with Morgan's grandmother when they were young girls. As a result, Prudence loved to harass and berate the Blackmoore girls in public. Morgan's eyes darted around the room, looking for an escape route.

"Just who do you think you are?" Prudence demanded, her hands fisted on her hips, legs spaced shoulder width apart. Morgan noticed she was wearing her usual knee high rubber boots and an orange sunflower scarf.

Morgan's brow furrowed over her ice blue eyes as she stared at the older woman's prune like face.

"Excuse me?"

"Don't you play dumb with me Morgan Blackmoore. What kind of concoction did you give my Ed? He's been acting plumb crazy."

Morgan thought back over the previous week's customers. Ed Littlefield *had* come into her herbal remedies shop, but she'd be damned if she'd announce to the whole town what he was after.

She narrowed her eyes at Prudence. "That's between me and Ed."

Prudence's cheeks turned crimson. Her nostrils flared. "You know what *I* think," she said narrowing her eyes and leaning in toward Morgan, "I think you're a witch, just like your great-great-great-grandmother!"

Morgan felt an angry heat course through her veins. There was nothing she hated more than being called a witch. She was a Doctor of Pharmacology with a Master Herbalist's license, not some sort of spell-casting conjurer.

The coffee shop had grown silent. Morgan could feel the crowd staring at her. She leaned forward, looking wrinkled old Prudence Littlefield straight in the eye.

"Well now, I think we know that's not true," she said, her voice barely above a whisper,

"Because if I was a witch, I'd have turned you into a newt long ago."

Then she pushed her way past the old crone and fled out the coffee shop door.

Fiona Blackmoore stared at the amethyst crystal in front of her wondering how to work it into a pendant. On most days, she could easily figure out exactly how to cut and position the stone, but right now her brain was in a pre-caffeine fog.

Where was Morgan with her latte?

She sighed, looking at her watch. It was ten past eight, Morgan should be here by now, she thought impatiently.

Fiona looked around the small shop, *Sticks and Stones*, she shared with her sister. An old cottage that had been in the family for generations, it sat at one of the highest points in their town of Noquitt, Maine.

Turning in her chair, she looked out the back window. In between the tree trunks that made up a small patch of woods, she had a bird's eye view of the sparkling, sapphire blue Atlantic Ocean in the distance.

The cottage sat about 500 feet inland at the top of a high cliff that plunged into the Atlantic. If the woods were cleared, like the developers wanted, the view would be even better. But Fiona would have none of that, no matter how much the developers offered them, or how much they needed the money. She and her sisters would never sell the cottage.

She turned away from the window and surveyed the inside of the shop. One side was setup as an apothecary of sorts. Antique slotted shelves loaded with various herbs lined the walls. Dried weeds hung from the rafters and several mortar and pestles stood on the counter, ready for whatever herbal concoctions her sister was hired to make.

On her side sat a variety of gemologist tools and a large assortment of   crystals. Three antique oak and glass jewelry cases displayed her creations. Fiona smiled as she looked at them. Since childhood she had been fascinated with rocks and gems so it was no surprise to anyone when she grew up to become a gemologist and jewelry designer, creating jewelry not only for its beauty, but also for its healing properties.

The two sisters vocations suited each other perfectly and they often worked together providing customers with crystal and herbal healing for whatever ailed them.

The jangling of the bell over the door brought her attention to the front of the shop. She breathed a sigh of relief when Morgan burst through the door, her cheeks flushed, holding two steaming paper cups.

"What's the matter?" Fiona held her hand out, accepting the drink gratefully. Peeling back the plastic tab, she inhaled the sweet vanilla scent of the latte.

"I just had a run in with Prudence Littlefield!" Morgan's eyes flashed with anger.

"Oh? I saw her walking down Shore road this morning wearing that god-awful orange sunflower scarf. What was the run-in about this time?" Fiona took the first sip of her latte, closing her eyes and waiting for the caffeine to power her blood stream. She'd had her own run-ins with Pru Littlefield and had learned to take them in stride.

"She was upset about an herbal mix I made for Ed. She called me a witch!"

"What did you make for him?"

"Just some Ginkgo, Ginseng and Horny Goat Weed ... although the latter he said was for Prudence."

Fiona's eyes grew wide. "Aren't those herbs for impotence?"

Morgan shrugged "Well, that's what he wanted."

"No wonder Prudence was mad...although you'd think just being married to her would have caused the impotence."

Morgan burst out laughing. "No kidding. I had to question his sanity when he asked me for it. I thought maybe he had a girlfriend on the side."

Fiona shook her head trying to clear the unwanted images of Ed and Prudence Littlefield together.

"Well, I wouldn't let it ruin my day. You know how *she* is."

Morgan put her tea on the counter, then turned to her apothecary shelf and picked several herbs out of the slots. "I know, but she always seems to know how to push my buttons. Especially when she calls me a witch."

Fiona grimaced. "Right, well I wish we *were* witches. Then we could just conjure up some money and not be scrambling to pay the taxes on this shop and the house."

Morgan sat in a tall chair behind the counter and proceeded to measure dried herbs into a mortar.

"I know. I saw Eli Stark in town yesterday and he was pestering me about selling the shop again."

"What did you tell him?"

"I told him we'd sell over our dead bodies." Morgan picked up a pestle and started grinding away at the herbs.

Fiona smiled. Eli Stark had been after them for almost a year to sell the small piece of land their shop sat on. He had visions of buying it, along with some adjacent lots in order to develop the area into high end condos.

Even though their parents early deaths had left Fiona, Morgan and their two other sisters property rich but cash poor the four of them agreed they would never sell. Both the small shop and the stately ocean home they lived in had been in the family for generations and they didn't want *their* generation to be the one that lost them.

The only problem was, although they owned the properties outright, the taxes were astronomical and, on their meager earnings, they were all just scraping by to make ends meet.

All the more reason to get this necklace finished so I can get paid. Thankfully, the caffeine had finally cleared the cobwebs in her head and Fiona was ready to get to work. Staring down at the amethyst, a vision of the perfect shape to cut the stone appeared in her mind. She grabbed her tools and started shaping the stone.

Fiona and Morgan were both lost in their work. They worked silently, the only sounds in the little shop being the scrape of mortar on pestle and the hum of Fiona's gem grinding tool mixed with a few melodic tweets and chirps that floated in from the open window.

Fiona didn't know how long they were working like that when the bell over the shop door chimed again. She figured it must have been an hour or two judging by the fact that the few sips left in the bottom of her latte cup had grown cold.

She smiled, looking up from her work to greet their potential customer, but the smile froze on her face when she saw who it was.

Sheriff Overton stood in the door flanked by two police officers. A toothpick jutted out of the side of Overton's mouth and judging by the looks on all three of their faces, they weren't there to buy herbs or crystals.

Fiona could almost hear her heart beating in the silence as the men stood there, adjusting their eyes to the light and getting their bearings.

"Can we help you?" Morgan asked, stopping her work to wipe her hands on a towel.

Overton's head swiveled in her direction like a hawk spying a rabbit in a field.

"That's her." He nodded to the two uniformed men who approached Morgan hesitantly. Fiona recognized one of the men as Brody Hunter, whose older brother Morgan had dated all through high school. She saw Brody look questioningly at the Sheriff.

The other man stood a head taller than Brody. Fiona noticed his dark hair and broad shoulders but her assessment of him stopped there when she saw him pulling out a pair of handcuffs.

Her heart lurched at the look of panic on her sister's face as the men advanced toward her.

"Just what is this all about?" She demanded, standing up and taking a step toward the Sheriff.

There was no love lost between the Sheriff and Fiona. They'd had a few run-ins and she thought he was an egotistical bore and probably crooked too. He ignored her question focusing his attention on Morgan. The next words out of his mouth chilled Fiona to the core.

"Morgan Blackmoore ... you're under arrest for the murder of Prudence Littlefield."